Starring the Baby-sitters Club!

**Other books by
Ann M. Martin**

Ma and Pa Dracula
Yours Turly, Shirley
Ten Kids, No Pets
Slam Book
Just a Summer Romance
Missing Since Monday
With You and Without You
Me and Katie (the Pest)
Stage Fright
Inside Out
Bummer Summer

BABY-SITTERS LITTLE SISTER series
THE BABY-SITTERS CLUB series
THE BABY-SITTERS CLUB mysteries
(see back of the book for a more complete listing)

THE BABY-SITTERS CLUB

Starring the Baby-sitters Club!
Ann M. Martin

AN
APPLE
PAPERBACK

SCHOLASTIC INC.
New York Toronto London Auckland Sydney

Reprinted with permission of Charles Scribner's Sons, an imprint of Macmillan Publishing Company, from *Peter Pan* by James M. Barrie. Copyright 1911, 1921 by Charles Scribner's Sons; copyright renewed 1939, 1949 by Lady Cynthia Asquith and Peter Llewelyn Davies.

Interior illustrations by Angelo Tillery

Cover art by Hodges Soileau

ISBN 0-590-45661-X

12 11 10 9 8 7 6 5 4 3 2 1   2 3 4 5 6 7/9

Printed in the U.S.A.   40

First Scholastic printing, December 1992

*For Brian Selznick,
a rising star*

STONEYBROOK

Stoneybrook Middle School
Presents
PETER PAN

Tryouts open to all elementary,
middle school, and high school
Students.

Audition date will be posted
at a later time.

TUTORING

Basketball Game

PROLOGUE

Jessi

J ust when I think my life couldn't be any more wonderful, guess what happens. Two more wonderful things! Oh, all right, let's face it. Nobody's life is perfect. But I didn't say mine was perfect. I said it was wonderful. And it is — when I ignore the not-so-wonderful parts — like the fact that I am one of the few African-American kids in my school (for that matter, in my town), which sometimes is *not* easy.

But I figure I've more than made up for the difficult and sad times with all that wonderful stuff. For instance, I have a wonderful family. I live in Stoneybrook, Connecticut, with my mother and father, my younger sister Becca (she's eight; I'm eleven), and our baby brother Squirt. (His real name is John Philip Ramsey, Junior.) The sixth member of my family is Aunt Cecelia, Daddy's sister. Sometimes she's a pain, but mostly she's okay.

Jessi

I have wonderful friends; six, as a matter of fact. They are the members of the Baby-sitters Club, or the BSC. (I'll tell you about that later.) And one of them is my best friend, Mallory Pike. Mal is eleven and in sixth grade at Stoneybrook Middle School (SMS) with me.

And I'm involved in some wonderful activities. As you might expect, I baby-sit. A lot. (What else would a member of something called the Baby-sitters Club do?) Then there's ballet. Ballet is my passion. I have studied for years, and I take classes at a special dance school in Stamford, which is the nearest big city to little Stoneybrook. I had to audition just to get into the school. Not to brag, but I have earned leading roles in several of the productions put on by my school. And I have danced in lots of ballets. My teacher, Mme Noelle, tells me, "Work hard and zen harder, and someday I sink you weel donce wiss a major ballet company." (Mme Noelle speaks with a French accent, in case you couldn't tell.)

So. What are the two more wonderful things that happened? Well, they happened at SMS on the same day. First, I learned that I had been chosen as the sixth-grade correspondent for the *SMS Express*, our school newspaper. When I first thought about writing for the paper, Mama said to me, "Jessi, you're going to

2

over-extend yourself." (My real name is Jessica, but hardly anyone ever calls me that.) I thought about what Mama said. I was already pretty busy, what with dance classes and baby-sitting and schoolwork. Then I pictured myself over-extended, my body like rubber, my arms and legs and head stretching out wildly in five directions. And then I talked to Emily Bernstein, who's the student editor of the *SMS Express*. Emily told me that each correspondent is responsible for just one article a month, a round-up of student activities. I decided I could handle that, so I submitted some writing samples to Emily, and today she told me I had officially been named the sixth-grade correspondent.

Well, as if that weren't enough wonderfulness, guess what I found out about five minutes after I heard Emily's news? I was walking to the cafeteria and on a wall in the hallway I saw a poster announcing that SMS — my very own school — was going to be putting on a musical extravaganza, *Peter Pan*. Anyone could try out for any role. The date of the auditions was to be announced.

All *right*! This was awesome! *Peter Pan* would be my chance to shine in front of all the kids at SMS. My friends in the BSC had seen me in performances at my dance school, but the other kids hadn't. Now I could show everyone what I can do. I could show them the real Jessi Ramsey. Plus, I was just perfect for the part of Peter Pan. For one thing, that part is usually played by a female. For another, Peter Pan has to be able to dance (not to mention fly), and I had plenty of stage experience.

I was so excited about being the sixth-grade correspondent *and* Peter Pan, that a fabulous idea sprang into my mind. I decided to ask Emily if I could write a special article about the play for the *SMS Express*. I would cover the extravaganza from start to finish as an insider. I would write about auditions, rehearsals, and opening night. I would write about the hopes and dreams of the cast members. I could be an on-the-spot reporter.

Even though I was on my way to the cafeteria for lunch, I suddenly decided I was too excited to eat. What an amazing turn my life had taken. (How lucky can you get?) I did an about-face in the hallway and ran to my locker. I pulled out a notebook and checked my purse to make sure I had a pen. Then I dashed to the library, sat down at an empty table, opened the notebook, and began scribbling ideas for my article. Even at that early stage I felt bad for the kids who were going to audition for the role of Peter Pan and lose out,

4

but I tried not to worry about them. Maybe they would even make a good angle for the article. Coping with disappointment and that sort of thing.

Today, I wrote in my notebook, *marks the beginning of* Peter Pan, *the musical extravaganza of SMS, and I am here to report on it.*

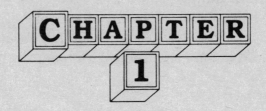

CHAPTER 1

Jessi

Monday

My wonderful day just kept getting wonderfuller (fuller of wonder?) I got the go-ahead for the article on <u>Peter Pan</u>. So now I better keep daily notes. I want to give the play full coverage.

Jessi

*B*rrrring!

The last bell of the day rang, and a kid in my eighth-period class jumped to his feet and yelled, "Okay! School's over!"

"For the *day*, just for the *day*," said our teacher, smiling. "I'll see you all tomorrow, same time, same place."

I slammed my notebook closed and ran for the door. The thing is, I really like school. And I work hard and do well (most of the time). Usually, I leave class like a normal person, not a racehorse. But on that day I couldn't wait to catch up with my friends and talk to them about *Peter Pan*. Oh, and tell them about my new job on the *SMS Express*.

I tore through the hallways, dodging kids like a football player, and approached my locker so fast I nearly crashed into it.

"Jessi!" exclaimed a voice. "Where were you at lunch today?"

Mallory Pike was standing next to my locker, looking worried.

"Oh, in the library," I answered. "I was too excited to eat. I have great news!"

"You were so excited you had to go *study*?"

"I wasn't studying. I was working on a project. Wait till we meet up with the others. Then I'll tell everyone the story at once."

Jessi

"This is very mysterious," said Mal.

Mal has been my best friend ever since my family moved here from New Jersey. That was back at the beginning of sixth grade. Now I feel as if I've been in Stoneybrook forever, even though I haven't been here long at all. At least, not long compared to kids like Mal who were born here. Maybe that's one reason I was so eager for the kids at school to see me as Peter Pan and get to know the real Jessi. To a lot of them, I was just "the new girl." (And to some of them, I was "the new black girl.")

Anyway, Mal and I have a lot in common, which is probably part of the reason we're best friends. We love children (what a surprise), and we're each the oldest kid in our family. However, while I have just one brother and one sister, Mal has four brothers and three sisters. They range in age from five to ten. (Three of the boys are identical triplets.) Also, Mal and I both love to read, especially horse stories. And we both wish our parents wouldn't treat us like such babies. Oh, well. Maybe they're improving a little. They finally allowed us to have our ears pierced. But Mal still wants to wear contacts instead of her glasses, and her parents will not budge on the matter.

8

One big difference between Mal and me is that Mal has no interest in ballet. I mean, she likes to *go* to the ballet sometimes, but she wants to be a writer when she grows up. And maybe an illustrator. She likes art and sewing and things like that.

When Mal and I had gotten our coats out of our lockers we flew to the front entrance of SMS and stood breathlessly just outside the door. Immediately, Mal started stamping her feet and hugging herself. She is always cold.

"Mal, it's like forty-five degrees or something," I told her.

"Practically the Arctic," she replied through chattering teeth.

"Hey, you guys!" The door banged open and out streamed Kristy Thomas, Claudia Kishi, Dawn Schafer, Stacey McGill, and Mary Anne Spier, the older members of the BSC.

"Hi!" replied Mal and I, and I added, "Guess what!"

But before I could continue Kristy said, "Did you see the sign about *Peter Pan*? Isn't that exciting?"

"Yeah. In fact — "

"I might try out for it," Kristy continued.

"Me, too," said Dawn and Stacey.

"Well, I — " I started to say.

"And did you read what it said about other

kids trying out for parts?" asked Claudia.

I paused. "What other kids?" I asked.

"Kids at the high school. Kids in the elementary schools. They want a few older kids to play some of the grown-up roles, and a bunch of little kids to be the Lost Boys and the Indians. I guess," replied Claudia. "I didn't read the poster very carefully."

"I bet Karen will want to be in the play," said Kristy. (Karen is Kristy's seven-year-old stepsister. She is very lively and loves being the center of attention.)

I cleared my throat and looked around at my friends.

"I think," said Mal, raising her voice slightly, "that Jessi would like to make an announcement or something." (Ordinarily, Mal and I take a backseat when we're around our BSC friends, since they are older than us — thirteen and in eighth grade — but Mal could tell I was ready to explode.)

"What is it?" asked Kristy. Kristy likes to think she's our leader.

"Well," I began, "today Emily Bernstein told me I was picked to be the sixth-grade correspondent for the *Express*."

"Hey, congratulations!" cried my friends.

"Thank you," I said. Then I continued. *"And I had this great idea to ask Emily if I could*

10

also write a special article about *Peter Pan*. I could cover the play from start to finish. As an insider."

"What do you mean, as an insider?" asked Claud.

"You know, as someone who's behind the scenes."

"Like an on-the-spot reporter?" suggested Mal.

"Exactly!" I exclaimed. Sometimes I think Mal can read my mind. "I'll be perfect for the job. Who's more on-the-spot than Peter Pan, after all?" (My friends were staring at me.) Before they could jump down my throat, I said, "I know, I know — playing Peter Pan and writing an article at the same time will be a lot of work, but I think I can handle it."

Nobody said a word.

"Don't you think it's a good idea?" I asked finally.

"Well," said Mary Anne, "I guess, um, I mean . . . Jessi, how did you get to be Peter Pan already? The date of the auditions hasn't even been announced."

"Yeah," said Kristy, frowning.

"Oh, well, it isn't official," I replied. "But who else would get that part? I'm a dancer, I have plenty of stage experience, and Peter Pan is usually played by a woman."

12

"But it's an important role. Don't you think an eighth-grader might get it?" asked Mary Anne gently. (She is the most sensitive, tactful person I have ever met.)

"I think the person who's best for the part will get it," I told her.

"I bet it goes to a high school kid," said Kristy.

"Who knows?" said Dawn. "Practically everyone in school is going to try out for the play. This is the biggest thing that's happened at SMS in years . . . isn't it?" (Dawn hasn't lived in Stoneybrook much longer than I have.)

"I'll say it is," agreed Claudia.

An awkward pause followed. The silence was broken when Stacey said, "So is everyone ready to go? I'm getting cold standing here. My toes are turning numb."

"Mine lost feeling ten minutes ago," said Mal.

"Well, my room awaits you," announced Claud grandly.

The BSC holds its meetings in Claudia's bedroom. Our meetings don't start until five-thirty, but sometimes, when we don't have plans or sitting jobs, we hang around together beforehand.

I had started across the lawn with my

Jessi

friends when I noticed somebody standing at one of the school bus stops. It was Emily Bernstein.

"Hey, there's Emily!" I cried. "I have to talk to her. You guys go ahead. I'll meet you at club headquarters later."

I changed direction and dashed over to Emily.

"Hi, Jessi," she said pleasantly. Emily is an eighth-grader. She's sort of friends with Stacey and Claud.

"Hi," I replied. And all of a sudden I felt shy about my idea. "Um, um," I began. "Um, could I ask you something?"

"Sure," said Emily. She was scanning the parking lot for her bus.

"Okay. You know *Peter Pan*? I mean, you know the play SMS is going to put on? The musical extravaganza?"

"Yeah?"

"Well, I'm going to be . . . to be in it. I mean, associated with the production. And I was thinking I could write an insider's article covering it from beginning to end. Auditions, rehearsals. You know."

Emily paused. "Oh, you're the *dancer*," she said after a moment. "Of course you'll be in the play. I see. Yeah, an article about *Peter Pan*

14

would be excellent, especially coming from an insider. Okay. Go for it, Jessi."

"Thanks! You won't be disappointed!" I exclaimed.

I thought about the play and the article all the way to Claud's house. Let's see. I was sure some of my friends would be in the play. I could ask them to keep daily notes about things that happen. Notes would be useful. . . .

Kristy

Monday BSC meeting

Keeping daily notes about anything is not my favorite activity, but I will do it for Jessi and her article on Peter Pan. I've certainly asked my friends to keep notes for me and my projects often enough. Anyway, at the moment there isn't a lot to say about the musical extravaganza. The date for the auditions hasn't even been announced. Still, excitement is running high here in BSC head-quarters.

Whent my friends and I (minus Jessi) reached Claud's bedroom after school that day, the entire rest of the afternoon stretched ahead of us. That doesn't happen often. Usually we're so busy that we scatter in all directions — baby-sitting, going to classes or lessons or appointments — and we just barely manage to gather for our club meetings.

The Baby-sitters Club was my idea and, if I may say so, it was a pretty good one. Actually, the club is a business. And very successful. The members meet three times a week on Monday, Wednesday, and Friday afternoons from five-thirty until six. During the meetings, parents call us to line up baby-sitters for their kids. With seven of us to answer the phone, the parents are bound to find a sitter with just one telephone call. That's a nice arrangement, which is probably why the BSC is so successful. Well, it's part of the reason. The other part is that my friends and I are responsible sitters and we run our club responsibly. As president, I see to that.

I'm Kristin Amanda Thomas, known as Kristy, and I come from a big, jumbled-up, happy family. I live with my mother, my stepfather Watson, my three brothers, my adopted sister, my grandmother, and sometimes my stepbrother and stepsister. (And a floppy puppy, a cranky cat, and two boring goldfish.) My brothers are Charlie and Sam who go to Stoneybrook High School, and David Michael who is seven and in second grade. My adopted sister is Emily Michelle, who's Vietnamese. She's two and a half. And my stepbrother and stepsister are Andrew and Karen Brewer, Watson's kids. They are four and seven, and live with us parttime. (The rest of the time they live at their mother's house.)

Some things about me that you should know are that I'm outgoing and active and have been called a loudmouth. I love children and sports and I coach a softball team for little kids. I don't care much about clothes or fashion or boys, but every now and then I go out with this guy in my neighborhood. His name is Bart Taylor, he's exactly my age — and he coaches a rival softball team. Some people might call Bart my boyfriend, but that's just a matter of semantics.

My BSC job is to run our meetings and to come up with most of the ideas for running the club efficiently. Thanks to me, my friends and I have an up-to-date notebook full of important information about our clients, and appointment pages where we can record sitting jobs. We also have a treasury that we keep full by paying weekly dues. The money in the treasury covers our club expenses.

Of course, I do not have to do all this work myself. That's where my friends come in. The vice-president of the BSC is Claudia Kishi, whose room we regularly use for club meetings. Claud and I grew up across the street from each other, until Mom got remarried. After the wedding, Watson moved my family across town and into his (huge) house. But before that, Claud and I saw each other nearly every day of our lives.

Claudia is Japanese-American. Her family consists of her, her parents, and her older sister Janine the Genius. The important things to know about Claud are that she loves children, junk food, and art, and is a talented artist. She does not love school and does not do well in it. Claud is striking looking and is something of a fashion plate at SMS. She's known for her wild clothing and hair styles. Sometimes she leans toward the outrageous, particularly where jewelry is concerned. She makes a lot of her own jewelry and, well, you sort of have to see it to believe it. Anyway, Claudia is the BSC VP mostly because she has her own phone *and* her own personal phone number. This is important because during our club meetings we don't get calls for other people, and we also don't worry when we tie up the phone for half an hour.

Mary Anne Spier is the secretary of the club and also my best friend. For years, she lived next door to me (and across the street from Claud). We played together endlessly, even though we are about as different as two people can be. Mary Anne is shy and quiet and sensitive. She cries over things like those commercials for the telephone company. And she grew up with just her dad. She has no brothers or sisters, and her mother died when Mary Anne was a baby. Recently, though, there have been big changes in her life. Mr. Spier got remarried and Mary Anne now has a stepmother, stepsister, and stepbrother. (Sound familiar?) However, the unusual thing about this is that Mr. Spier married the divorced mother of Mary Anne's other best friend. So Mary Anne's best friend became her stepsister. And wait'll you hear who her best friend/stepsister is. Dawn Schafer. A BSC member. After the marriage, Mary Anne and her dad and her kitten Tigger moved into the Schafers' old farmhouse. Mary Anne had a family at last (not that she and her father by themselves weren't a family, but you know what I mean), *and* Mr. Spier began to change. He used to

20

overprotect his daughter terribly, but now he's loosened up. He's allowing Mary Anne to grow up.

Mary Anne's job as club secretary is to keep our notebook and appointments in order, and to schedule the baby-sitting jobs. She's excellent at this. Also, she has very neat handwriting.

I might as well tell you about Dawn Schafer next, since you already know something about her. Dawn was born in California, but moved to Stoneybrook with her mother and brother Jeff after her parents got divorced. This was not too long ago, in the middle of seventh grade. Then, as I said, her mom fell in love with Mr. Spier and they were married. And *then* Jeff moved back to California to live with his father. This was not because of Mary Anne and her dad. Jeff had simply never adjusted to the move to Connecticut, and he wanted to return to the place he thought of as home. Dawn was sad about that, of course, but she has coped. Dawn is a survivor. She's also very independent. She does what she wants and what she believes in, whether it's dressing in her own style, or sticking to her healthy diet. No junk food for Dawn. No red meat, either. Dawn just adores things like sprouts and tofu and macrobiotic foods. Yuck. There must be some diet that falls in between Claudia's and Dawn's.

Dawn is the alternate officer of the BSC. Whenever one of us has to miss a meeting, Dawn can take over the duties of that person. She's like a substitute teacher, I guess.

Stacey McGill is the club treasurer and Claudia's best friend. Honestly, those two were made for each other. Stacey (who's a little boy-crazy, and at the moment is going out with my charming brother Sam) is just as wild a dresser as Claudia. Well, actually, Claud may be a bit flashier than Stacey, but Stacey is a bit more sophisticated, so they even out. Stacey has this wild blonde hair that she keeps getting permed, and she dresses as if she just stepped out of the pages of a fashion magazine.

Stacey's life is not all lipstick and boys, though. It's much more complicated (and, frankly, more interesting). Stacey was born and raised in New York City. She moved to Stoneybrook at the beginning of seventh grade, when the company for whom Mr. McGill works transferred him. Not long after that, the McGills decided to divorce, so Stacey wound up in Stoneybrook with her mother, while her father is back in NYC. Like Mary

Anne, Stacey is an only child. And she doesn't even have a pet. Sometimes I think Stacey and her mom are a little lonely, even though they have good friends in Stoneybrook. All in all, Stacey's life is not easy right now. On top of everything else, she has diabetes, a disease with which she has to cope every day and for the rest of her life. Sometimes she doesn't feel very well, and every now and then she winds up in the hospital, but mostly you'd never know Stacey is sick. (My mother refers to her as a "trooper.")

Remember the treasury I mentioned? Out of which we pay club expenses? I make it sound like such a big deal, but the "treasury" is just a wrinkled old manila envelope. However, the contents are important, and Stacey is in charge of it. She collects our dues once a week, and doles out the money as needed, watching over things to make sure the treasury is never empty. (By the way, Stacey is a math whiz, which helps considerably.)

Okay. I know Jessi has already introduced herself to you, as well as Mallory Pike. What she didn't mention is that she and Mal, the two younger members of the BSC, are junior officers of the club. Basically, this means their parents will not yet allow them to sit at night, even on weekends, unless they're at home

23

watching their own brothers and sisters. However, Mal and Jessi, who are excellent babysitters, are extremely important to the BSC since, by always taking on day jobs, the rest of us are freer to handle evening jobs. In fact, the seven of us are an awesome team.

If you can believe it, there are times when, awesome or not, seven of us are not enough sitters. Every now and then a job's offered to the BSC that not one of us is free to take. When that happens, we call on our associate club members. Our associate members are Logan Bruno and Shannon Kilbourne. Logan is . . . *ta-dah* . . . Mary Anne's steady boyfriend. They've been going out for months now (after Mr. Spier allowed it), and they're a perfect couple, I think. Shannon lives across the street from me in my new neighborhood. The associate members do not attend club meetings. But they are responsible sitters we can call on in a pinch.

Jessi showed up in Claudia's room that Monday afternoon not too much later than the rest of us. She'd only needed to talk to Emily for a few minutes, she said. And she told us that Emily had liked her idea for the article about *Peter Pan*. And *then* she asked us to keep notes in order to give her lots of material for the article. None of us minded doing that. Not really.

"So what are you guys talking about?" Jessi wanted to know, as she settled herself into her usual spot on the floor next to Mal.

"What else? The play," Stacey answered. "The more I think about it, the more excited I get. I've never been in a musical extravaganza. I don't want to be a great actress one day or anything. I just think being in this play would be really fun."

"Ditto," I agreed.

"Ditto," said Dawn.

"Not," said Mary Anne. "You will not catch me anywhere near the stage, the auditorium — "

"What a surprise," I said, and Mary Anne giggled.

"You know what? I bet some of my brothers and sisters will try out for the play," spoke up Mal.

"Hey, mine too," I said.

"Definitely Karen," added Jessi.

"And probably some of the kids we sit for," said Claud.

"I wonder which parts will go to the high school kids," said Mary Anne.

"I wonder which high school kids will try out," said Stacey.

Kristy

Claud arched an eyebrow. "Maybe Sam will," she said pointedly.

Stacey threw a pillow at Claud, and Claud threw it back at her.

Soon an all-out pillow fight was underway. However, several minutes later I had to announce, "It's five-thirty. Please come to order."

CHAPTER 3

Dawn

Tuesday

Today we found out that the auditions for the play are going to be held on Saturday. That's just four days from now! You'd think we'd get a little extra time to prepare for the parts we want. On the other hand, I overheard this one teacher say he's going to be looking for "raw talent." Still... four days. Four days until maybe (just maybe) I will have earned the part of Tiger Lily.

Dawn

"What *is* this goo?" asked Kristy. She was holding up something from her lunch tray. It was gray and stringy. "It looks like what Watson's cat might bring in — "

Kristy was stopped by a shriek. "Don't!" cried Mary Anne. "Do not start, Kristy. Please. You are going to make me sick."

"I'm already sick," said Kristy. She was still holding up the stringy thing. "I can't believe this was actually *in* my *lunch*."

"Put it down, okay?" said Mary Anne weakly.

Kristy obeyed. Then, surprisingly, she continued eating her lunch.

I returned to mine, too. However, mine was not a school lunch. I had brought it from home. I always do. And I had packed it myself. Fruit salad, bean salad, a packet of raisins and raw cashews, and a box of sugar-free juice. Sometimes kids make fun of me for carrying a lunch to school. However, *I* never have to worry about stringy things that look like the cat brought them in.

It was Tuesday, the day after my friends and I had heard about the musical extravaganza, and Kristy, Mary Anne, Stacey, Claud, and I were sitting at our usual table in the cafeteria. Jessi and Mal don't eat with us, since the sixth-graders have lunch during a different period. However, Logan had joined us. He joins us about half the time. The rest of the time he eats with his guy friends.

Once we had settled down (and once Kristy had hidden the stringy thing in a napkin), we began talking about *Peter Pan*.

"Guess what," said Claud. "I decided what I want to do in the play."

"You want to be in it?" asked Stacey. "I didn't know you wanted to be in it."

"Well, not *in* it, exactly. I want to work on the scenery. Wouldn't that be fun? Think of the sets for *Peter Pan*. The nursery, Neverland, the pirate ship. Painting the scenery would be totally cool."

"Oh, you'll be great at that, Claud," I said. "I'm sure whoever is in charge of the scenery would die to have you work on it."

Kristy looked up from her lunch. "I'm going to try out for the part of Nana," she announced.

"Nana?" repeated Logan. "That big dog?"

"Nana isn't just any dog," Kristy replied. "She watches over Wendy, Michael, and John like a regular nanny."

"But she's still a dog. You'd have to wear a sheepdog costume."

Kristy grinned. "I know."

"Hey!" exclaimed Mary Anne. "Last night Dawn and I were looking through the program for *Peter Pan* — we saw the show in Stamford, remember? — and we noticed that the person who played Nana also played the crocodile."

"The crocodile that bit off Captain Hook's hand?" asked Claudia.

"Yup," I said.

"Well, that would be okay," said Kristy. "Another cool costume. In Nana's costume I could galumph across the stage. In the crocodile costume I could slither across the stage."

I giggled. This was so Kristy. Leave it to her to want the animal roles.

"I still don't know what part to try out for," said Stacey, looking worried. "I really don't. I just want some small role. Can I go to the auditions and say that? Or will that sound too, you know, uncommitted? I mean, I really don't care what part I get as long as I can be in the play. I don't even have to have a speaking role."

"I think that's okay, Stace," I said. "Just tell them what you said right now. You want to be in the play no matter what role you get. Maybe you'll really impress everyone. Maybe you'll wind up as Peter Pan."

"Nope," said Claud. "That's Jessi's part."

Mary Anne smiled. "Where did Jessi get that

idea? She does know she has to audition on Saturday, doesn't she? She doesn't *really* think the role is already hers."

"Oh, she knows she has to audition," Stacey replied. "But I have this horrible feeling she thinks it's just a formality, that the director is ready to give her the part no matter who tries out for it."

"Maybe she's right," said Logan.

"Maybe," I agreed. "She certainly does have stage presence. And experience. And she certainly can dance. We've all seen her."

"Can she sing?" asked Mary Anne.

"As well as the rest of us, I guess," said Stacey.

We paused, each thinking about Jessi. After a few moments Mary Anne said, "Tell them what you decided, Dawn."

I blushed. "We-ell . . ."

"Come on, tell us," Kristy urged me.

"I decided to audition for the part of Tiger Lily."

"That's a pretty big part," said Stacey.

"I know. That's the problem. I don't really think I'll get it. But it would be a lot of fun."

In *Peter Pan*, Tiger Lily is the Indian Princess in Neverland who is also Peter's friend. She gets to sing a couple of great numbers, including the "Ugg-a-Wugg" song with Peter and the Indians. And of course she gets to wear a pretty exotic costume.

"Hey, Logan," said Kristy. "Do you want to be in the play?"

Logan nodded, and swallowed a mouthful of mashed potatoes. "Yup, but I'm like Stacey. I don't know what part I want. I don't even really care. Maybe one of the pirates or something."

"You know what Mal told us on the way to school this morning?" I said. "She wants to work on costumes. I think she'd be good at that. I mean, she's always — "

"*Shh!*" Kristy interrupted me. She elbowed my side.

"Kristy!" I yelped.

"Shh," she said again, but more quietly. She cocked her head toward the table next to ours, and I peered around her to see who was sitting there. "Don't be so *ob*vious!' she cried, but then noticed that the rest of our friends were now looking at the other table. And everyone at the other table was now looking back at us. Kristy buried her head in her hands. "You guys could never be spies," she said.

Here's who was sitting at that other table. Cokie Mason, Grace Blume, and their friends. They are mortal enemies of the BSC. We are always getting involved in arguments or playing tricks on each other. They don't like us and we don't like them. You know what? I can't even remember why. But our feud continues.

"What's going on?" Logan whispered to Kristy.

"Guess who's trying out for Tiger Lily," she replied.

"Dawn is," said Mary Anne.

"No. Guess who *else* is trying out. Cokie."

"Oh," I groaned. "You're kidding. I don't want to compete with Cokie."

"It figures she'd want the part of an Indian princess," said Claudia. "She already is a princess."

"Dawn, you're still going to try out for Tiger Lily, aren't you?" asked Mary Anne. "Don't let Cokie stop you."

I made a face. "I don't know. Being involved with Cokie — in any way — is so unpleasant. Plus, I don't want to beat her and I don't want her to beat me. If I beat her, she'll make my life miserable. If she beats me, I'll never hear the end of it. So either way, I lose."

"Dawn, don't you dare not try out just because of Cokie," said Kristy. "You are not a quitter. And since when do you care what other people think of you?"

"It's not so much what she thinks," I answered. "It's what she'll do. You guys know very well what she's done in the past." Everything from scaring us to death to trying to steal our boyfriends.

My friends and I returned to our lunches, even though I was pretty sure Cokie and Grace were now whispering about us. Probably they were plotting horrible, terrifying deeds. However, I tried to concentrate on our own conversation, and I turned toward my sister.

"A bunch of the Pike kids are definitely going to try out," Mary Anne was saying. "Mal told us this morning."

"Charlotte refuses," spoke up Stacey. "I knew she would." Stacey often sits for Charlotte Johanssen, who is a wonderful kid, but very shy.

"I'm with Charlotte," said Mary Anne. "I bet Becca Ramsey won't try out, either." Jessi's little sister is as shy as Charlotte, which may be why they're best friends.

"I talked to Karen last night," said Kristy. "She has her heart set on Tinker Bell. I hope she won't be disappointed. I tried to tell her that Tinker Bell isn't an actual person. She's not really a character in the play. But . . ."

I couldn't help it. My mind drifted from our conversation back to the one at Cokie's table. Maybe I wouldn't try out for the play after all.

CHAPTER 4

Stacey

Saturday

Audition day. I knew I shouldn't be nervous. I wasn't trying out for some role I wanted desperately, like Jessi was. Or even like Kristy was. She would not give up on Nana and the crocodile. I didn't even want a big role. Still, I was going to have to stand on the stage in the auditorium by myself and read lines from the script. Worse, after that I was going to have to sing by myself.

Stacey

On Saturday morning, Mom drove me to SMS. Going to school on a Saturday morning seemed pretty strange. But I was too keyed up to think about that.

I hesitated before opening the car door and climbing out.

Mom turned off the engine. "Do you want me to come in with you?" she asked. "Just for moral support? I'll stay entirely in the background. No one will know your mother is there."

I smiled. "Thanks," I said. "Actually, I would sort of like you to come in. I wouldn't even care if the kids knew. But I feel I should do this on my own. I should be a grown-up."

"Are you sure?"

"Positive."

"You're already more grown-up than most thirteen-year-olds," said Mom. "You don't have to prove anything."

"I know. But . . . well, anyway, my friends will be there. We'll all give each other moral support. I think I can do this, Mom."

"Okay, honey." Mom started the engine. "Break a leg!" she called as I opened the door.

I waved to her and ran inside.

The auditorium was a madhouse. Kids everywhere. High school kids, middle school kids, elementary school kids, and some kids so young they must have come to the auditions because their older brothers or sisters were going to try out. I saw a bunch of parents, too, and grouped at one end of the stage, a handful of teachers.

For a moment I just stared at everyone. Then slowly I took off my coat and gloves, and unwrapped the scarf from around my neck. I left my things on a seat in the back row and approached the chaos near the stage. I knew Mallory must have arrived already because I saw Nicky, Margo, Claire, and the triplets — all of her brothers and sisters except Vanessa, who probably was not interested in auditioning. I also saw Karen Brewer, David Michael Thomas, a bunch of kids I've baby-sat for, Cokie, Grace . . . and Sam Thomas.

"Sam!" I called, and ran to him.

"Hi, Stacey!" he replied. Sam held out his arms, but the second we reached each other, he pulled them back. And I drew away from him. I knew we were thinking the same thing. How were we supposed to greet each other in public? We hadn't been going out seriously for too long, and only a few people (namely, the other members of the BSC) had seen us together. I wasn't sure Sam's friends even knew about me. High school guys did not often date middle school girls.

"Um," I said, "um, I didn't know you were going to be here."

"I didn't decide to come until this morning. It's a zoo at our house this weekend — Karen and Andrew are with us — and at breakfast nobody could talk about anything except the play. By the way, Kristy, Karen, and David Michael are here somewhere. Anyway, during breakfast Brian called. You know, my friend Brian?" (I didn't know, but I nodded my head, and Sam continued.) "He said he's going to try out for the part of Captain Hook, and some of our other friends are going to audition, so I decided to come along." He paused to catch his breath. "Why are you here? I mean, what are you auditioning for?"

"I haven't made up my mind," I told him. "Any little part."

Kristy ran to us then, and pulled at my elbow. "Stace! Everyone's here! We're all in the front row. Come sit with us. . . . Oh, hi, Sam," she added, as if she'd just noticed her brother.

Some guy I didn't know (Brian maybe) called to Sam, so I went off with Kristy. "See you later, Stace!" said Sam.

I followed Kristy to a section of the front row. Sure enough, the entire BSC was sitting there. Even Mary Anne.

"Mary Anne!" I exclaimed. "I didn't expect to see you here."

"I didn't expect to *be* here," she replied. "I am here for moral support only. This is as close as I get to the stage. Did everyone hear me?"

"Mary *Anne*," said Kristy. "Chill out."

I sat next to Claud, near the end of the row. Presently, Mr. Cheney, one of the teachers, stepped to the center of the stage. "May I have your attention, please? I am Mr. Cheney, the director of *Peter Pan*. If you are here to audition for the play, please take a seat in the front of the auditorium."

During the next few minutes, Mr. Cheney organized the chaos and explained how the auditions would work. I paid attention to him, breathing deeply in an attempt to relax. The younger children, he said, were going to audition first. That made sense, since most of them already could not hold still, and they'd only been at SMS for a few minutes.

"All right. Kids ten and under, please come to the stage."

After a brief stampede, the stage was crowded with elementary school kids. I realized I knew about half of them, mostly from baby-sitting. When they were holding as still as they were able, Mr. Cheney said, "We need you younger kids to play the parts of the Lost Boys, the Indians, and Michael Darling. Girls may be Indians and Lost Boys, but we do need a boy to play Michael. It is — "

"Excuse me! Excuse me!" called a high voice, and one of the kids wriggled out of the crowd and stood at Mr. Cheney's feet.

It was Karen Brewer. Kristy looked like she wanted to crawl under her seat.

"Excuse me, sir?" said Karen. "What about Tinker Bell?"

"What about her?" asked Mr. Cheney.

"I want to be her."

"But Tinker Bell isn't a character. We simulate her . . . I mean, we, um, we'll just make . . . fairy sounds to show that Tink is around."

"But I want to be Tink! I WANT TO WEAR A FAIRY PRINCESS COSTUME! *I WANT TO* — "

Kristy decided she better rescue poor Mr. Cheney. In a flash she was running across the stage. "Sorry," she said breathlessly as she grabbed Karen by the hand and led her to the back of the crowd of kids. While she talked to her sister, Mr. Cheney and Ms. Halliday divided the children into two groups. (Ms. Halliday is a gym teacher.) Mr. Cheney helped one group memorize a short scene in the play. Ms. Halliday taught the other group a dance routine. After awhile, the groups would switch places. Meanwhile, a third teacher, Mr. Drubek, handed scripts to us older kids so we could learn the lines for the parts we were interested in. I was about to raise my hand and ask, "What if we don't know which part to read for?" when Mr. Drubek said, "If any of you is undecided, please learn a page of Peter Pan's lines after the 'I've Got to Crow' number in Scene One. And if you have a question, just ask me."

I flipped through Scene One until I found the spot Mr. Drubek meant, and I read a couple of pages. Meanwhile, Kristy had calmed Karen down and sent her to join one of the groups of children. For quite a while the auditorium was filled with odd sounds — kids murmuring to themselves or humming the songs they planned to sing, and (onstage) a lot of stamping and jumping from the kids working with Ms. Halliday. Before I knew it, though, the teachers were ready to begin the actual auditions.

The auditorium fell silent. Mr. Cheney consulted a clipboard. "Matt Braddock!" he called, and two kids stepped to the front of the stage.

They were eight-year-old Matt and his older sister Haley. My friends and I sit for them a lot. I knew why Haley was with Matt. Matt is

41

profoundly deaf and communicates using sign language. Haley was going to interpret for her brother.

Haley introduced herself to Mr. Cheney. Then she said, "Matt is deaf. He can't talk so he can't sing. But he's a good dancer. Please could he try out for something without talking? Is there some character who doesn't have to say any lines?"

"Of course," replied Mr. Cheney. "No problem." Then he asked Haley to ask Matt to look angry, then excited, then scared, and so forth. Matt was a pro. (And no wonder. Sign language is very expressive.)

"Thank you," said Mr. Cheney finally, and he grinned at Matt. Then he consulted his clipboard again. "Karen Brewer."

When Karen ran to the front of the stage and Mr. Cheney saw who she was, he turned slightly pale. Then he recovered himself. "Have you learned the part?" he asked her. (He managed to smile.)

"Yup."

Karen read the part with Mr. Cheney. When they had finished, she said, "Want to see how I can be a fairy?"

"Well — " began Mr. Cheney.

Karen didn't wait for an answer. She hopped around the stage while Mr. Cheney turned desperately toward Kristy. And Kristy rescued him again. This time she picked Karen up, carried her offstage, and made Karen sit in her lap while the auditions continued.

Mallory's brothers and sisters took their turns. So did David Michael. So did Buddy Barrett and Jake Kuhn and Myriah Perkins and Hannie and Linny Papadakis and Nancy Dawes and a bunch of other kids my friends and I sit for.

I wondered if Mr. Cheney got as tired as I did of hearing those same lines spoken over and over and over. Just when I thought I couldn't take any more, Mr. Cheney said, "Thank you, kids. Ms. Halliday and I will watch you dance now. In your groups. Group one, please."

Kristy finally released Karen, saying, "No fairy stuff, is that clear?" Then she returned to my friends and me. We sat forward in our seats and watched the dancers eagerly. We watched Buddy, who never missed a step. We watched Karen, who showed off, ending her steps with flourishes and hand gestures. And we watched Jackie Rodowsky, our walking disaster, stumble from the beginning to the end of the routine. At least he had read well — very well. I hoped that would make up for his two left feet. I knew he wanted to be in the play.

By the time the little kids were finished, I had nearly forgotten that I would soon be up on that stage auditioning. But I snapped to attention when Mr. Cheney dismissed the little kids. Sometime later, when he called, "Stacey McGill," I nearly had a heart attack.

CHAPTER 5

Jessi

Saturday

I wowed Mr. Cheney at the audition. I know it. Mr. Halliday too. I think all my friends did well today. Including Stacey. I don't know what she was so nervous about. And Dawn did better than Cokie. I'm glad she decided to try out for Tiger Lily after all. I think she'll get the part. I hope Kristy gets these animal roles. I think Mr. Cheney

Jessi

was surprised
that anyone
specifically wanted
to be Nana and
the crocodile. He
had to ask her
to read those
lines of Peter's so
he could get a
better sense of
her as an actress.
What a day.
I'm exhausted.

As the little kids were leaving the stage and
finding their parents in the back of the auditorium, Mr. Cheney said, "Auditions for
smaller parts first, bigger parts later." He was
talking to those of us still waiting to perform.
"If you are prepared with a dance routine and
a song, fine. If not, please see Ms. Halliday.
Everyone must read, dance, and sing today so
we can see the full range of your talents."

I watched the kids who surrounded Ms.
Halliday then. Thank goodness I wasn't one
of them. I was prepared. After reading for the
part of Peter I was going to perform a dance

46

I had choreographed myself and sing "I'm Flying." I had learned the entire song, even though I knew Mr. Cheney wouldn't need to hear all of it.

Let's see. I could talk forever about the auditions, but I better just give you the highlights. I'll start with my BSC friends. The first one of us to face Mr. Cheney was Stacey, who looked kind of shaky. But I have to admit that when she read her lines she was good. Very good. Her song was good, too. (She sang the first few lines of "Mack the Knife," which was strange, but Mr. Cheney didn't seem to mind.) And then she said she was going to perform Ms. Halliday's dance routine later, along with the rest of the kids who hadn't prepared in advance. After that she rushed off the stage.

Kristy did pretty much the same thing, except that she read even better than Stacey did, and she sang part of "I Won't Grow Up" from Act II.

"Good going," I told her as she returned to her seat. "Nice breath control. And you looked at the audience a lot. Just try not to tense up your muscles so much. It makes you seem nervous."

Kristy gave me a funny glance. "I don't think anyone will be able to tell once I'm inside the sheepdog costume," she said.

Sheesh. Touchy.

The pirates auditioned next. Among them were Logan and Sam. They both read for the part of this pirate named Bill Jukes. I wondered how badly they both wanted to be Jukes. Because if Logan's heart was set on it, he was going to be disappointed.

I leaned around Kristy and said, "Stacey! Stacey!" in a loud whisper.

"Yeah?"

"Sam is great. He'll get the part of Jukes for sure. No contest. He's *good*, Stace. I didn't know there was so much talent right here in little Stoneybrook." Not that I'd ever lived anywhere except in small towns, but you know what I mean. I leaned around in the other direction and peered at Mary Anne. I have to tell you that Logan's audition had not gone too well. He spoke his lines in a loud, flat monotone, barely pausing at commas or periods. He seemed to have forgotten the purpose of punctuation. His singing had not been much better. He could carry a tune okay, but that was about all. He kept messing up the words to "Wendy." Instead of singing, "We have a mother! At last we have a mother!" he sang, "We have another! At least we have another!" And for, "Wendy's waiting at the door, we won't be lonely anymore," he sang,

"Wind is wading on the floor, we won't be lovely anymore." Now does that even make sense? I could only hope that Logan would make up for it during the dancing later. Maybe he would be, like, this incredible show dancer.

On the stage Mr. Cheney was clapping his hands for attention. "Who is going to audition for Tiger Lily?" he asked.

"Oh, my lord," I heard Dawn whisper. "I don't know if I can go through with this." She glanced around the auditorium, looking for Cokie Mason, I guess. The older BSC members had told Mal and me what had happened during their lunch period last Tuesday, but I thought that was forgotten. I thought Dawn had decided not to let Cokie bother her.

"Dawn! Get up on that stage!" hissed Kristy. "If you don't, you will never forgive yourself." She paused. "You will die wondering, 'Could I have been Tiger Lily? Could I?' You could blow a career on the stage if you don't get moving. Just forget about Cokie."

Sometimes it's a good thing Kristy is so pushy. Dawn jumped to her feet. She marched up the steps to the stage. She never looked back. And she was the first to try out for Tiger Lily.

Dawn was great. She was fan*tas*tic. She was so much better than my friends and I had

49

imagined that we just kept looking at each other with raised eyebrows and open mouths. She read her lines, she sang a verse of the "Ugg-a-Wugg" song . . . and then she danced. I was sure she was going to dance with Ms. Halliday's group later, but instead she performed this very sweet waltz. She performed it by herself, but she did it so realistically I could have sworn she was actually dancing with a partner.

Okay. That was the good part about the auditions for Tiger Lily.

The bad part was that Cokie performed just as well as Dawn did. Mr. Cheney was going to have a tough choice to make.

I looked at my watch. I looked at the list of parts kids would try out for before Mr. Cheney was ready to see the Peter Pans. I would not be on that stage for a while. But I was not nervous. I was well-prepared and I knew it. Ever since Monday I had practically been living in Neverland. My parents had found this old record album of the songs from *Peter Pan* and I had listened to it endlessly. I had watched the video of Mary Martin playing Peter Pan in the TV adaptation of the stage play. Actually, I had watched it nine times. This was for two reasons. One, I was studying Mary Martin's dancing. Two, Squirt suddenly decided "Pan" was his new favorite video, and he kept asking to watch it. By asking I mean that he would plant himself in front of the nearest grown-up at our house and say, "Pan, Pan, *Pan*, PAN, *PAN!*" until the grown-up dashed for the VCR in order to save his or her eardrums.

I felt as if I had been sitting in the front row of the auditorium for a year when Mr. Cheney finally said, "And now, tryouts for the part of Peter Pan. And the rest of you, remember — don't go anywhere. Ms. Halliday still needs to see most of you dance. After that, we're going to call back about ten of you to hear you one final time. We'll make our decisions in several days. The parts will be posted by the office here at school, but everyone will be notified by phone as well. Okay, Peter Pans. Up on stage!"

I bolted out of my seat and reached the stage before anyone else did. "Hi, Mr. Cheney, remember me?" I said. "I'm Jessi Ramsey."

Mr. Cheney is not one of my teachers, but he got to know all the BSC members pretty well on a memorable school trip. During a time of extra bad winter weather all of SMS went to this ski lodge in Vermont for a week. The lodge was gigantic, and other school kids were there, too. One was a group of elementary children from Maine who ended up needing baby-sitters while they were there. (It's a long story.) Anyway, my friends and I volunteered, which impressed the SMS teachers, especially Mr. Cheney.

"Oh, Jessi. Yes, of — "

"And I'm the dancer, remember?" I interrupted him. "I take ballet at the school in Stamford. I've played Clara in *The Nutcracker* and I've starred in *Coppélia* and *Swan Lake* and *Sleeping Beauty*."

"Thank you, Jessi," said Mr. Cheney. "All right, please — "

"Plus, I've — "

"Jessi, a résumé isn't necessary. Are you ready to read?"

"Yes, sir. And to sing and dance. I've choreographed a routine."

"For now, please just read."

I read. And I was good. Maybe not as good as I would be when I danced, but I was good. When I finished I sang "I'm Flying," which also went well, although I thought I saw Grace Blume out in the audience with her hands over her ears, but what would you expect from a mortal enemy of the BSC? Anyway, so maybe I'm not exactly an *operatic* singer, but I was going to make up for everything when I danced. Which was now. At last

Jessi

I could demonstrate my dancing ability.

I had arranged a number with a lot of leaps and tour jetés and things in it so Mr. Cheney and Ms. Halliday would be able to imagine how I would look when I was flying over the stage on wires. That's how they do it, you know. I mean, that's how they simulate the flying in *Peter Pan*. Peter, Wendy, Michael, and John are attached to strong, practically invisible wires in the scenes in which they fly. They can go from walking across the stage to flying over it in one smooth movement. Then, still connected to the wires, of course, they can swoop and glide and even dance in the air.

Anyway, I finished my performance and turned hopefully toward Mr. Cheney, but all he said was, "Thank you, Jessi. Madeline Carver, you're next." So I walked into the wings and watched the other Peter Pans, who included two boys. They were good, but not great.

When Mr. Cheney had seen the Peter Pans, Ms. Halliday worked with the dancers for awhile, and then came the announcement I was waiting to hear. All us kids had returned to our seats. Mr. Cheney faced us from his place on the stage and said, "Okay. Thank you very much, everybody. You've been wonderfully patient. You, too!" he called for the benefit of the few parents who were seated in the back rows. "Now would the following people please stay behind for another hour or so. Franklin Enell, Dawn Schafer, Sam Thomas, Kristy Thomas," (he was interrupted here by a burst of cheering) "Jennifer Abrams, Stacey McGill, Cokie Mason," (more cheering) "Roger Bucknell, Alan Gray, and Rick Chow."

Dawn clutched at my elbow. "Is this good or bad, Jessi?" she squeaked. "He called my name. Is that good or bad?"

"Oh, it's very good," I assured her. I smiled. "Mr. Cheney wants to see you again. It means you impressed him."

"Oh." Dawn smiled back, but then she frowned. "He didn't call *your* name, Jessi."

I patted her arm. "I know. Don't worry about it." Of course Mr. Cheney hadn't called my name. He'd already made up his mind about the role of Peter Pan. I left the auditorium feeling pleased and confident.

CHAPTER 6

COKIE

FRIDAY

THAT LITTLE ~~TWERP~~ JESSI RAMSEY ASKED ME TO GIVE HER NOTES ABOUT BEING IN THE PLAY OR SOMETHING. I'M REALLY NOT SURE WHAT I'M SUPPOSED TO DO. SHE'S ONLY A SIXTH-GRADER AND I SHOULDN'T HAVE TO PAY ATTENTION TO HER AT ALL. ON THE OTHER HAND, SHE IS WRITING A BIG ARTICLE FOR THE SCHOOL PAPER AND I'M PRACTICALLY THE STAR OF THE SHOW.

I had to summon every ounce of my maturity to ignore Cokie's remarks about my status at SMS. But I will not play her games.

When I write my article about the play, I will not mention that she called me a twerp (even if she crossed it out) or that she thinks I'm "only" a sixth-grader. And I will call her a conceited jerk only when I am talking about her with the other members of the BSC.

I was sitting in my eighth-period class with Grace Blume when we heard the news. Grace and I manage to have more than the usual number of classes together every year. We arrange this in September. We wait until we receive our class schedules. Then we compare them. And then we start talking to our teachers, our guidance counselors, and even the principal, if necessary. We say things like, "You know, I'm really my freshest in the morning. I'm sure I'd do much better in math if I could switch from sixth period to second period. To Mr. *Zorzi's* second-period math class." By the time we've finished switching we usually have three or four classes together. This year we have five. It is a record. We are proud of it.

Anyway, we were sitting in the back row of our social studies class passing notes back and forth about what's going on with *General Hospital*, the soap we started watching last year. If one of us has to miss it, the other takes notes. We try to catch each other up during school, before the next episode comes on. I had passed Grace a note, she'd passed one back with a question, I'd answered it, and she was working on another question when an alien note appeared on my desk. It had come from Ellie Szilagyi who sits right in front of me. Ellie's not a good friend or anything, but she's okay. I think she would like to hang around with Grace and me, but so far we haven't let her. Maybe when her complexion clears up.

Ellie's note said: *The parts have been posted!!! There on the wall by the office. Try to beet the crowd!!!!!*

I was so excited I didn't even bother to correct Ellie's spelling. I just passed the note to Grace. After she read it we were both so excited we didn't even bother to write down the homework assignment. What we did instead was very quietly organize our books and backpacks so that when the bell rang we were immediately able to leap to our feet and run out of the classroom. That was how we managed to be two of the very first SMS students to see who had earned which roles in the play.

"Find Tiger Lily! Find Tiger Lily!" I cried to Grace, who was already running her finger down the list.

"Okay, I'm trying!" Grace was as excited as I was, even though she hadn't tried out for the play. "Here it is. Tiger Lily."

"Oh, my lord! I'm dying. Read what it says! I can't bear to look."

"It says . . . Cokie Mason! Cokie, you got it!" screeched Grace.

"Oh, my lord!" I cried again.

Finally I dared to look at the list with my own eyes. First I found Tiger Lily. I wanted to see my name for myself. Not that Grace would trick me or anything, but you never know. Then I started at the top and began to read the whole list. This was not easy since a crowd was gathering behind me and everyone was pressing against me like a wave.

The first part listed was Peter Pan. I ran my finger along the line to the name Kristy

Thomas. "Kristy Thomas!" I shrieked. I grabbed Grace's elbow. "Kristy Thomas is Peter Pan!"

Grace's face fell. *"What?"* she said in this flat voice. "I do not believe it. I mean, actually I do. That girl gets everything."

"But she's never acted before," I pointed out.

"And anyway, didn't she want to be that alligator?"

"Crocodile," I corrected Grace. "Oh, well. Let me see. Who got to be Wendy?" I peered at the list again, but by then someone was in front of me. I stood on tiptoe trying to see over the blonde head. "Wendy," I murmured. "Wendy will be played by — "

"Me!" exclaimed the voice belonging to the blonde head. It was Dawn Schafer. "Me! I'm Wendy!" Dawn paused. Then she said, "How'd I get to be Wendy? Who's Tiger Lily? I can't find it."

"*I* am Tiger Lily," I said.

Dawn turned around slowly. "Figures," she replied and walked away.

I tried to gloat. After all, I'd gotten what I wanted, hadn't I? I was going to be Tiger Lily and Dawn wasn't. On the other hand, Dawn was going to play *Wendy*. That role was much bigger than the role of Tiger Lily. Wendy is onstage during most of the play. She's in every act, and she has tons of lines and musical numbers.

By this point I was losing my spot before the list on the wall. Several more kids had squeezed in front of Grace and me, and others were surging around us on both sides. One of them was Claudia Kishi. A bunch of her friends must have been somewhere behind us, because she stood there forever, shouting out names for them to hear.

"Logan, you're going to be a pirate!" she yelled.

"All *right!*" I could hear him yell back. "Which one?"

"I don't know. Oh, wait. It looks like Noodler. Is there a pirate named — Oh! Oh, my lord!"

"What? What is it?" yelped Logan.

"Stacey and Sam!" Claudia began to giggle. "Stacey and Sam are going to be Mr. and Mrs. Darling!"

"We're *what*?" shrieked Stacey. "Claud, I bet you didn't read that right."

"I did, too. . . . Where is Kristy? We have to tell her the news."

"Oh, please, Claud. Don't broadcast it. Everyone will know soon enough."

"Not the news about *you*. The news about

her. She doesn't know she's Peter Pan yet. At least I don't think she does."

"Hey, there she is!" called someone in the crowd. "Kristy, you're Peter!"

"What?"

"You got the part of Peter Pan!" said Claudia.

"But I wanted to be Nana and the crocodile," Kristy wailed. (What a brat.)

"Claudia?" spoke up a hesitant voice nearby. "Um, did Jessi get a part?"

"Oops. Good question, Mal."

Claudia turned back to the list, and I remembered that the little twerp Jessi Ramsey had gone on and on at the auditions about what a great dancer she is. She had wanted to play Peter Pan. And Kristy Thomas had gotten the part. Ooh, this would make trouble in the baby-sitting club.

"Jessi's a pirate," said Claudia, more quietly. "Where is she, anyway?"

Apparently, no one knew. Finally Stacey said, "Keep going, Claud. Who else has parts? Is Jackie Rodowsky in the play?"

"Hey! Jackie's going to be Michael Darling! And Karen is going to be Tinker Bell. How did that happen? There is no Tinker Bell."

"Maybe Mr. Cheney changed his mind," said Logan.

"Who got the parts I wanted?" asked Kristy.

"Pete Black did," replied Claud. "Hey, David Michael's in the play, too. He's one of the Lost Boys. Oh, my lord, Alan Gray gets to be Smee, that funny pirate. And we know a whole bunch of the Indians and Lost Boys. Myriah Perkins, Mal's brothers and sisters, Matt Braddock. Matt's an Indian! Great! He'll love that!"

"Who's Captain Hook?" asked Stacey.

"Some name I don't know. Maybe a high school guy?"

"Excuse me," I said, pushing forward and jostling Claudia. "Are you finished hogging the list? Other people might want to see it."

"Okay," said Claudia pleasantly. "I think you'll be interested in the second page."

"The second page? What second page?"

"The one under the first," Claudia answered witheringly. Then she stepped away.

The crowd was thinning out. I lifted the first sheet of paper to find one labeled CREW. And I was about to say, "Who cares about the crew? Those are the boring jobs," when I caught sight of Claudia's name. It was listed after Set Designer. I kept reading. The only other name I cared about was listed after Apprentice Costume Designer. The name was Mallory Pike.

Oh, no. One member of the BSC was going

65

to be in charge of the scenery behind me? And another was going to work on my costume? They better make me look good, I thought. If they didn't . . .

"Yo, Mallory Pike, " I said loudly. She had started to drift off with her friends, but she turned around. "You better do a good job on my costume," I warned her. "You better make me look good."

"Leave her alone, Cokie," said Kristy Thomas.

I ignored her. "And Claudia, *you* better do a good job on the scenery. If anything goes wrong I'm going to blame you — "

"Oh, shut up," Claudia interrupted me.

But I thought she looked just the teeniest bit worried.

CHAPTER 7

Claudia

Firday

Firday was confussing. Most of my friends
were in the play or working on it just
like they wanted but not just like they
wanted. What I mean is Kirsty wanted to be
in the play she wanted to be the cook took
animals only she got Peter pan. Jessy whanted
to be peter but shes a pirate. Stace wanted to
be in the play but she did not whant to be
Sam's husbend. The thing about me is I just
whanted to paint senery not be the set Desiner.

67

Claudia

Well, I had a feeling we were going to be in for it at the club meeting that afternoon and I was right. By five-thirty, after the news about the play had had a chance to sink in for real, my friends and I were fairly emotional. All week we'd been waiting and hoping. We'd been wondering, Did I get the part or didn't I? Or, will I really be able to work on the scenery? Now we were confused by these unexpected turns of event. As you might imagine, we didn't do much work at the meeting. I mean, we answered the phone and scheduled jobs (we *have* to do that), but in between we talked only about the play. Mostly, we talked about Kristy and Jessi.

"It's unbelievable, that's what it is," said Kristy, after we had given her official BSC congratulations. (We were trying to be sensitive to Jessi, but we did want Kristy to know we were proud of her.)

"Aren't you happy, Kristy?" asked Mary Anne.

"I — I don't know yet. I wanted to wear those animal costumes. I never thought about being something else. Especially not Peter Pan."

"But now you have the part," said Dawn. "So how do you feel?"

68

"I don't have any experience singing or dancing *or* acting."

"I'll say," muttered Jessi.

"I guess you just have raw talent," said Stacey. "Mr. Cheney and Ms. Halliday must have been impressed with your audition. They called you back, and then they gave you this big part. They must think you can handle it. And they should know. They're the experts."

Jessi snorted. As usual, she was sitting cross-legged on the floor. She and Mal always do. But on that afternoon she had separated herself from everyone. She would barely look at us. We decided to leave her alone for a while. We figured she'd simmer down on her own and then start talking to us. So we didn't comment on her snort.

"Being Peter Pan *is* sort of exciting," said Kristy finally. "I just wasn't expecting it. I kind of like to be prepared for things. But I am flattered . . . and also really scared. Hey, I found out about Karen and Tinker Bell. I talked to Karen's mother this afternoon. She told me Mr. Cheney called and said he decided to make Tinker Bell an actual character after all. Maybe Karen's flitting around paid off. Anyway, I do think she'll make a good Tinker

Bell. Put her in a fairy costume and she'll be thrilled."

"Is David Michael excited?" asked Dawn.

"Definitely. And Sam is — " Kristy broke off, glancing at Stacey. Then she changed the subject. "Well, guess what," she said. "Andrew has decided he feels left out. Now he desperately wants to be in the play. But he's too young. Too bad the cutoff age is five."

"Guess what happened at my house this afternoon," spoke up Mal. She was trying just a little too hard to sound happy and amusing. I figured this was for Jessi's benefit, since Jessi wouldn't talk even to Mal. "I was feeling so relieved that the cutoff age was five, because it meant Claire wouldn't be left out of the play, and then there was her name on the list at school. She was going to be an Indian, along with Margo and the triplets. And Nicky is going to be a Lost Boy. And Vanessa doesn't want to be in the play, so everybody's happy, right? Wrong. Claire says she will not be in the play unless she can wear a beautiful costume. I think she means a princess costume. She says she will not dress up like an Indian and she especially will not dress up like a boy."

"So?" I asked.

"So she decided not to be in the play."

"You're kidding."

"Nope. My mom had to tell Mr. Cheney this afternoon."

"Oh!" said Kristy. "I almost forgot. I made lists of the little kids who are playing the Lost Boys and the Indians before I left school today. I think we'll need the lists. We know most of the names on them."

"Really?" said Mary Anne.

"Yup. Listen to this. Well, let me see. Let me take Claire's name off first. Okay. Indians — Hannie Papadakis and Nancy Dawes — they're Karen's best friends — Margo and the triplets, Matt Braddock, Buddy Barrett, and Kerry Bruno." (Kerry is Logan's younger sister.) "The Lost Boys — David Michael, Nicky, Myriah Perkins, Shea Rodowsky, Linny Papadakis, Carolyn Arnold, Melody and Bill Korman, Bobby Gianelli, and Natalie Springer. Bobby and Natalie are two of Karen's classmates, remember?"

From the end of my bed came this huge sigh. Dawn.

"What's the matter?" asked Mary Anne, immediately worried.

"Well, I mean, I know I should be honored to be playing Wendy, and I am, but I'm also scared to death. I'm like you, Kristy. I didn't try out for the part I got. And Wendy is a *huge* role. You know, you and I have the two biggest parts in the play."

This comment prompted another snort from Jessi.

"I'm scared, too," I said. "How did I wind up being the set *designer*?"

"I wasn't scared until Cokie came after me," said Mal. "I wanted to work on the costumes and that's what I'm going to do. But now I have to do it with Cokie breathing down my neck."

"Oh, for heaven's sake, you guys!" exploded Jessi.

"What? What's the problem?" I said testily. (I told you we were feeling a little emotional that afternoon.)

"What's the *prob*lem? Are you guys listening to yourselves? I guess not. This is what I'm hearing. You all *wanted* to be in the play, and now you all *get* to be in the play — mostly in even better ways than you imagined. Stacey, you tried out for any old part and you're going to be Mrs. Darling. Dawn, you tried out for Tiger Lily and you're going to be the female lead. Mal, you wanted to work on costumes and that's what you're going to do. Claudia, you wanted to paint scenery and you get to be set designer. And Kristy, you wanted to be some dog and you get to be Peter Pan." Jessi sounded like she might start to cry.

After a moment of silence Kristy said softly, "I'm sorry, Jessi."

More silence. Then Mal said, "Jessi, I know you wanted to be Peter Pan, but at least you're going to be an Indian. You know what? I'm a little relieved. You'll be able to keep an eye on my brothers and my sister. I have this feeling they're going to misbehave. So if you're a pirate — "

"Mallory. I am *not* going to be a pirate," said Jessi.

"But I thought — "

"Mr. Cheney listed me as a pirate, but that doesn't mean I have to play one."

"You're out of the play?" said Mal with a gasp.

"No. But I told Mr. Cheney I did not want some puny pirate role. I talked to him this afternoon."

"What did he say?" I asked.

"Well, he practically begged me not to leave the play."

I saw Kristy glance at Dawn. "He did?" she said.

"Yes. He asked me if I would please be the assistant choreographer. He desperately needs someone to choreograph simple dances for the children. I said I would do it."

"I wonder why Ms. Halliday can't — " I started to say, but Dawn nudged me with her elbow and I shut up.

"Jessi?" said Mal tentatively. "Did you ask Mr. Cheney why he gave you the part of a pirate?"

"Yes."

"Well, what did he say?"

"He said he wanted other kids to have a chance to perform. He said I've had a lot of starring roles already. He said . . . um, he said I'm too good for the part. . . . Yeah, that's what he said."

"Well, thanks a lot," said Kristy icily.

"Jessi, it *is* true you've been onstage a lot in your life and most of us haven't. I think Mr. Cheney's just trying to be fair," said Stacey.

Jessi snorted.

"Oh, be quiet. You sound like a horse," said Kristy.

And Jessi was quiet. After that she refused to say another word during the meeting. She wouldn't even look at anyone.

Except Kristy. The looks Jessi threw Kristy every now and then were murderous. I felt sorry for her. For Jessi, I mean. No wonder she felt so awful. She'd gone around saying she was going to play Peter Pan, and look

74

what had happened. Mr. Cheney had cast her as a pirate. On the other hand, if she hadn't been so cocky, if she hadn't *told* us she would be Peter Pan . . . Oh, well. You can't change the past.

When the meeting ended, I said good-bye to my friends, then sat on my bed and gazed out the window at the lights of the house next door. I thought about Cokie and her threat. What did she mean, I better make her look good? And what did she think she could do to me if I didn't? And what if I thought she looked good, but she disagreed?

You are being ridiculous, I scolded myself. Forget about Cokie. Concentrate on the scenery.

And that's exactly what I did do.

CHAPTER 8

Mary Anne

Wednesday

Today was the day of the first rehearsal for <u>Peter Pan</u>, although I'm not sure it was a rehearsal so much as an exercise in getting organized. But before I say anything more about the afternoon, let me tell you how I managed to get involved with the play in the first place. Remember I said I didn't want a thing to do with it? I didn't even want to be near the stage, let alone behind it or on it. Well, *guess what. I now have an official job and an official title, and I will be attending every single rehearsal along with the rest of my friends.*

"See you, Mary Anne!" called Logan.

"See you!" I called back. "I'll phone you tonight. 'Bye!"

Logan and I had walked partway home from school together, and we had reached the spot where we went off in different directions — Logan, to his house, and I, to the Braddocks' where I was going to sit for Haley and Matt. Actually, we were both going to be back at SMS shortly, but I didn't think we'd be able to spend any time together. Logan was going home long enough to pick up his sister, then take her back to school for the rehearsal. And I was going to take the Braddocks to the rehearsal. I planned to sit safely in the audience while Haley helped Matt backstage by translating for him. Logan and Kerry would also be backstage, preparing for their roles as a pirate and an Indian.

MaryAnne

Nothing went as I had planned.

When Matt and Haley and I reached SMS after a walk through damp, cold air that promised snow or maybe sleet, we hurried inside to the steamy warmth of the auditorium. The auditorium looked pretty much the way it had looked on the day of the auditions. Kids everywhere. Also jackets, mittens, gloves, scarves, hats, and boots. A few parents milled around, trying to keep track of the children and their gear. On the stage stood Mr. Cheney, Ms. Halliday, Mr. Drubek, and a couple of other teachers.

"This is a madhouse," I said.

"Where's Matt supposed to go?" wondered Haley.

And just then, Mr. Cheney called for the cast members to assemble backstage. "On the double!" he added. "Leave your coats and things out here on the seats, get your scripts, and please keep your voices down so you can hear further instructions."

The cast members — from five-year-olds to high school students — surged toward the steps to the stage in a great sea of bodies. Matt, following Mr. Cheney's directions which had been signed to him by Haley, began to follow the kids. And Haley began to follow Matt. But halfway to the stage she turned and looked at me, then back at the noisy crowd, then at me again. "Mary Anne?" she said. "Will you come with us?"

Go with them? To the world behind the stage? Was I crazy?

"Sure, Haley," I replied, and hurried to catch up with them.

After all, I was the baby-sitter.

But my heart was pounding and my stomach was doing flip-flops. I *was* crazy. First, I had gone to the auditions and sat *right near* the stage. Now I was at the rehearsal and I was going *back*stage. Next thing I knew I would have a role in the play.

"Hi, Mary Anne!" called a small voice as I joined the crowd of kids.

"Hey, hi, Mary Anne!" called someone else.

"Mary Anne, what are you doing here?"

I looked around. I was surrounded by baby-sitting charges — Margo and Nicky Pike, Myriah Perkins, Buddy Barrett, Carolyn Arnold.

"Hi, you guys," I replied. "I'm here with Haley and Matt. I'm sitting for them today."

"Attention. Attention, please!" Ms. Halliday was walking around, clapping her hands. "Pirates and Indians, listen up!"

"Indians. That's you, Matt," Haley signed.

The younger kids and the kids with smaller roles were being gathered into one area, while the kids with bigger roles were being gathered somewhere else. Jackie Rodowsky stood between the groups, looking confused. When he saw me, he ran to me.

"I don't know where I'm supposed to be," he whispered. "I'm just a little kid, but I have a big part. I mean — not to brag . . ."

"That's okay, Jackie," I said. "You're Michael Darling. You should be proud. Now let's find out where you belong."

I took Jackie by the hand. After he was settled with the proper group, I returned to Matt and Haley who were sitting on the floor near Ms. Halliday. Haley was signing quickly as Matt tried to watch both her and the teacher. I settled down next to them.

". . . your scripts," Ms. Halliday was saying. "Today I want you Indians to study your parts in the production. Read the stage directions. Older kids help the younger kids. You need to understand your role in the play."

Hannie Papadakis raised her hand. "Our role?" she repeated, frowning. "We're Indians. Aren't we?"

"Yes, of course," said Ms. Halliday. "What I meant was — "

"Ms. Halliday?" called Adam Pike. "When do we get our costumes?"

I stood up. "Ms. Halliday, I'll talk to Hannie for you," I said.

"Thank you," she replied, looking relieved.

I took Hannie aside and explained to her that Ms. Halliday was referring to the purpose and the actions of the Indians when they're onstage. As Hannie was rejoining her group, I heard an "oops."

The "oops" didn't sound very loud or even very urgent, but I could tell who it had come from, and I knew enough to be worried. I glanced around. "Jackie? Where are you?" I called softly.

"Over here," came the equally soft reply. "I mean, *up* here."

"Oh, lord," I muttered.

Above my head, clinging fiercely to a bunch of ropes, was Jackie Rodowsky, the walking disaster.

"What are you doing?" I hissed.

"Well, I got bored. I climbed up here to investigate and now I can't get down. But I have to get down because Mr. Cheney is talking to my group again. I don't want to miss anything."

"Jackie, these are not climbing ropes, like in gym," I told him. "They hold up scenery and stuff. If one of those ropes comes down, something else might crash down with it."

"Probably me," said Jackie ruefully.

I sighed. "You shouldn't be up there, you know that," I said. "But the important thing now is to get you down safely."

"Before Mr. Cheney sees," added Jackie.

"Right." I considered asking Logan or Kristy or someone for help, but everyone looked awfully busy. So I hauled a pile of tumbling mats underneath Jackie and told him to drop onto them.

"Okay," he said. Then, "Anchors away!"

Jackie landed safely on the mats. I helped him scramble to his feet. When we turned around we were facing Mr. Cheney.

"Uh-oh," muttered Jackie. He took a step sideways, tripped over his untied shoelace, stumbled backward against the mats, and slid to the floor. Before I could say a word, though, he had leaped to his feet again and was exclaiming, "It's okay! I'm not hurt!"

Jackie returned to the group of kids he was working with, leaving me facing Mr. Cheney. "Sorry about that," I said. "He's a little accident-prone. But he's a great kid. Honest. And he'll work hard. He wanted to be in the play more than anything."

"You know Jackie?" Mr. Cheney asked.

I nodded. "Yup. Really well. I baby-sit — "

"Mary Anne! I lost my shoe!" cried Karen Brewer, approaching me tearfully. "And I told Kristy, but she's too busy being Peter Pan."

"When did you take it off?" I asked her.

"I don't know. A little while ago. I felt something in it, so I sat down over there by those boxes," she wailed, pointing.

"Over there where that sneaker is?" I said.

"Oh, yeah!" Karen smiled through her tears and ran for her shoe.

I turned back to Mr. Cheney again, but was immediately interrupted by Haley. "Me and Matt need *help*!" she said desperately.

"Coming!" I replied. "Mr. Cheney — "

"You go ahead," he said. "We're both busy now. But Mary Anne, I'd like to talk to you after the rehearsal, if that's okay."

"Sure. I'm baby-sitting, but Matt and Haley can wait a few minutes."

Under ordinary circumstances, I might have worried. Why did Mr. Cheney want to talk to me? Was he mad at me for getting Jackie down by myself instead of asking for help? But I was far too busy to worry. During the rest of the rehearsal, kids kept coming to me with problems — ranging from lost scripts to loose teeth. Plus, I was a little distracted by Logan. He and the other pirates kept fooling around. Instead of studying their scripts, they held

83

sword fights using rulers. And they teased each other about their names. (Well, Noodler *is* a pretty silly name.)

Anyway, when the rehearsal ended, Mr. Cheney found me and said, "Mary Anne, you were an enormous help today. I don't know what we would have done without you. I was wondering — how would you like to come to every rehearsal and be our 'backstage baby-sitter'?"

I brightened. "I'd love to! Um, as long as I never have to set foot *on* the stage."

"It's a deal. Oh, one other thing. I think Jackie may need a little extra help — and supervision. Would you agree to be his personal coach?"

Of course I would. And I did.

Which was how I wound up involved with *Peter Pan* after all. Looking back, somehow it seemed inevitable.

CHAPTER 9

Mallory ⸛

Friday

When I pictured myself as the apprentice costume designer, I imagined sitting in a room somewhere backstage, surrounded by lengths of fabric, yards of lace, containers of sequins and beads. I would be seated at an ancient Singer sewing machine, piecing together a costume that I would later cover with sequins, sewn on by hand.

However, my first task as the apprentice costume designer was nothing like what I imagined. It was not glamorous. Furthermore, it was embarrassing.

Mallory ☺

As you know, Mr. Cheney had named me the apprentice costume designer. He had named an eighth-grader, Savannah Minton, the costume designer. Savannah and I were both working under Miss Stanworth, one of the home-ec teachers. (Miss Stanworth is young and glamorous. I've seen some of the stuff she's made — like all her own clothes —and it's really professional. I can't wait until Miss Stanworth is *my* home-ec teacher.)

At the end of the first rehearsal, Savannah (who doesn't go by a nickname, because the only one anybody can ever think of is Vanna, and she absolutely refuses) told me that at the second rehearsal our work as designers would begin. That was when I had that vision of creating wild, brilliant costumes in some forgotten backstage room. On Thursday, during lunch, I even decided to go exploring and find the room, but the band was rehearsing on the stage, and I didn't want to be discovered poking around. So I had to wait until Friday afternoon for my first assignment.

This was my first assignment. To measure the cast members. With a measuring tape. Even the boys.

I was supposed to go around measuring

boys? How, I wondered, was it going to be possible to measure boys without actually touching them?

You have to understand. There's nothing wrong with boys. I even *like* this one particular boy. His name is Ben Hobart. He's in sixth grade, he comes from Australia, and he was the apprentice lighting director on the play. Ben and I have gone to the movies a few times, and to a couple of dances, and sometimes we study together. Therefore, obviously, I have touched Ben a few times. Like when we were dancing and we held hands.

But measuring boys around their waists was a different story. First of all, some boys are jerks. I just knew that Alan Gray, the Pest of All the World, would give me a hard time. Plus, some of the cast members are in *high school*. How would Sam Thomas feel with Mallory Pike stretching a measuring tape around his waist?

"We have to measure all the cast members?" I repeated after Savannah had given me my assignment.

"Yes," she replied. "We want the costumes to fit."

"I know. Right. Sure we do. . . . Hey, I have an idea. How about if I measure all the girls and you measure all the boys?"

Savannah frowned slightly. "Why?"

"I don't know. I just thought . . . never mind."

"Look," said Savannah. "Measuring everyone is going to take awhile. My plan is to start with the people who have the biggest roles in the play or who have the most elaborate costumes. Like Kristy, because she's Peter Pan, and Pete, because he needs the Nana costume and the crocodile costume. Then we'll work our way down to the little kids who are playing Indians and the Lost Boys."

"Okay," I said in a small voice.

"So today I want to get measurements on all the kids with larger roles or fancier costumes. That's Liza the maid; John, Michael, and Wendy Darling; Mr. and Mrs. Darling; Pete Black for Nana and the crocodile; Tiger Lily; Peter Pan; Tinker Bell; Captain Hook; and Smee. If we can get to the other pirates, fine. If not, we'll measure them at the next rehearsal. Okay, Mal, I've divided this list in two. Here's your half. And here's a measuring tape. We need chest, waist, hips, hem lengths, and in some cases, other measurements. Those are described on the list. All right? Go to it."

Savannah hurried off. She left me standing backstage, holding the measuring tape. It dangled from my fingers. Kids were milling around me, but I barely noticed them. I didn't even hear them. I looked at the list Savannah had given me. This is what it said:

Dawn Schafer .... Wendy Darling

Jackie Rodowsky ...... Michael Darling

Karen Brewer .... Tinker Bell

Lucas Danver .... Captain Hook

Alan Gray .... Mr. Smee

Cokie Mason .... Tiger Lily

Beneath the names were descriptions of the costumes, their lengths, and so forth. (We needed to know whether the hem fell at the knees or the ankles, that sort of thing.) Some costumes were simple, such as Michael's nightshirt. Others were complicated, such as Captain Hook's pirate outfit.

I wondered who to start with. Maybe some-one easy, like Dawn, or even Karen Brewer. Then I realized I didn't know the kid who was going to play Captain Hook. Lucas Danver. Who was he?

"Kristy?" I called. I could see her reading from the script with Dawn. Since Kristy was Peter Pan, she ought to know who Hook was.

"Yeah?" replied Kristy. (Clearly, I had interrupted her.)

"Who's Lucas Danver?" I asked. "You know, the guy who plays Captain Hook?"

"I'm not sure. He goes to the high school. I think he knows Charlie."

Dawn had looked up from her copy of the script, too.

"Lucas Danver?" she repeated. "Kristy, he is only the most gorgeous guy at the high school. You do too know him. Remember at auditions? He was the one the girls cheered for after he finished reading Hook's part."

"Oh, yeah," said Kristy distractedly.

Kristy returned to the script, but I wanted to die. I had to measure the most gorgeous guy in the high school? This was getting worse and worse. I could not deal with the thought.

I decided to ignore the problem for awhile. "Dawn?" I said. "I have to measure you." I held up the tape. "It's my job."

"Okay. Kristy, I'll be back in a minute."

Dawn and I moved away from the action and I got to work. Nearby, Mary Anne, the backstage baby-sitter, was reading from the script with Jackie. She was holding Margo in her lap. Margo looked as if she'd been crying.

I abandoned Dawn.

"Margo?" I said. "What's the matter?"

"Hey!" cried Dawn. "Come back. Hurry up. I'm supposed to be reading with Kristy."

"Wait a sec. Margo's upset."

"It's okay, Mal," spoke up Mary Anne. "Margo bumped her knee, but she's fine now. She won't even have a bruise."

"Mary Anne, read with me!" commanded Jackie.

"Margo, are you really all right?" I asked.

Margo nodded, so I let Mary Anne go back to work with Jackie, and I finished measuring Dawn. When I had written down the information I needed, I placed a check by the name Dawn Schafer. I looked at the next name on the list. Jackie Rodowsky. I didn't think I should interrupt Jackie and Mary Anne again, so I moved on to Karen. Where was she? I glanced around backstage. I saw Ms. Halliday working with the Indians, Haley patiently translating for her brother. I saw Logan and the other pirates inventing a "pirate dance." (I don't know what they were supposed to be doing, but it wasn't that.) I saw Jessi trying to teach the Lost Boys (four of whom were girls) to execute a kick-step. And then I saw Adam, Jordan, and Byron, the triplets. I don't know what *they* were supposed to be doing, either, but they were hiding inside an immense cardboard box. It was large enough to have contained a washing machine. They had poked holes through the sides, and now they were blowing spitballs through the holes with pea-shooters.

I stuffed the tape measure in my pocket. I strode across the stage, pushing between Tiger Lily and one of the Indians, and I lifted the box right off the floor. Three pea-shooters went flying.

"Hey!" exclaimed Jordan indignantly.

"Hey, yourselves. You guys are supposed to be working with Ms. Halliday."

"We are not. She's working with the younger kids now."

"Well, you are not supposed to be shooting spitballs around the stage."

"Mallory, I will take care of this," said a quiet voice behind me.

It was Mary Anne. She did not sound (or look) pleased.

"Okay, okay," I replied.

"Hey, Mallory!" Savannah was walking briskly toward me. "How are you doing? Are you ready for another list?"

"Not quite."

"Okay. Who haven't you gotten to yet?"

"Well . . . Jackie, Karen, Lucas, Alan, and Cokie."

"*Mallory!*"

"I'm sorry."

Savannah did not sound (or look) very pleased herself. "Oh, here," she said. She tore my list in half, leaving me with the top. "I'll measure Lucas, Alan, and Cokie. Can you manage Jackie and Karen?"

I nodded. Relief flooded through me. I knew Savannah was upset with me, but at least (for now) I would only have to measure little kids.

Unfortunately, Savannah wasn't the only one upset with me. Mary Anne was no happier. "Mallory," she said, "*I* am the backstage baby-sitter. Please remember that."

CHAPTER 10

Dawn

Saturday

Tonight I had a brainstorm. It was about Wendy's character and her role in the play. I knew <u>Peter Pan</u> was going to be a little old-fashioned. After all, the first time it was produced was in 1904. But I didn't realize that the women's movement would figure so heavily into the story. Well, not exactly the women's movement, but the role of women in the story. If you play close attention to <u>Peter Pan</u> you'd never know there even was a women's movement, and I couldn't have that. I decided to do something *about it, since Mom always says to me, "Instead of complaining, do something."*

I decided to change Mr. Barrie's lines.

By Saturday, we had held two rehearsals. Neither one was quite what I thought of when I imagined a rehearsal. The characters were not on the stage reading their lines from the beginning of the play to the end. No, the rehearsals were much more basic. They were Ms. Halliday explaining to the kids the function of the Indians who, except for Tiger Lily, did not have speaking parts, although they had musical numbers. They were Mallory running around with her measuring tape. They were Karen trying to figure out how to portray a nonspeaking fairy who's usually seen simply as a shimmering light. They were Kristy and me reading our lines together, not yet even trying to memorize them, simply beginning to see what kind of energy we could create together.

However, at the end of Friday's rehearsal, Mr. Cheney did say we should begin to memorize our lines, that we would only be able to rely on our scripts for so long. On Saturday, Mary Anne offered to help me with that job.

Dawn

I guess she figured she was already more involved with the play than she had intended, so one more task wouldn't hurt.

"I'll read Peter's lines to you in your first scene," she offered, "and you see if you can come up with Wendy's."

That was exactly what we did. We sat side by side on my bed. The script was between us, so I could refer to it, but mostly I closed my eyes and tried to remember my lines.

"You know," I said after awhile. "Peter Pan has some nerve."

"What?" said Mary Anne.

"He's so selfish. The only reason he wants Wendy to come back to Neverland with him is so she can be a mother to him and the Lost Boys. He just wants someone who will cook and clean and sew for him."

"Wendy knows that. Peter Pan is very upfront with her."

"But he wants a maid!" I protested.

"Wendy doesn't have to agree to go. Anyway, Peter promised her and her brothers an adventure, didn't he?"

"Oh, that's just like a man," I replied. "They always say stuff like that. Those things are bribes. Sure, Peter promises Wendy an adventure. But he winds up with a maid, which is what he wanted in the first place. What a baby. First he loses his shadow. Then he can't even sew it on for himself, and how hard could that be? In the play, Wendy sews it back on in, like, ten seconds. Sheesh."

"Dawn, I think you're making too much of this. Anyway, so what if the play is sexist? It's been around since 1904 and everyone loves it and the story is a lot of fun."

"But what does the story say to little kids?" I countered. "It says boys should expect girls to do all the housework, and that isn't right. Look at your own father. He cooks and cleans. I've never seen him sew, but he makes up for it with the cleaning." (Mary Anne's father is like Felix Unger in *The Odd Couple*.)

"That's true. But . . . for heaven's sake, Dawn. Get a grip. This is a story with fairies and pirates and a magic land where people can fly and they never have to grow up. Why don't you just go with it? Anyway, what can you do about it? Drop out of the play?"

"No. I'm not going to drop out. But I'll think of something to do."

By the time Mary Anne and I went to the next play rehearsal, I had decided exactly what to do. And it did not involve dropping out of the play. (I wouldn't give Cokie the satisfaction.)

This was the first rehearsal at which the

characters stood on the stage and said their lines with each other. Not that we had costumes or even any scenery. And we didn't run through the entire play. We didn't even rehearse the scenes in order. We just waited for Mr. Cheney to call out, "Okay, now let me see the Darling children in Act One." (He loved referring to Wendy, Michael, and John that way.) Or, "And now I want to see Peter and Captain Hook," or Hook and Smee, or Peter and Tiger Lily, or whatever.

Halfway through the afternoon, Mr. Cheney called Kristy and me onto the stage. We stepped into the dim lights. We were wearing our school clothes and holding our scripts. Surprisingly, we had an audience. Scattered throughout the auditorium were teachers and kids who were interested in the progress of the play. I soon realized that we would have a small audience at every rehearsal.

"Kristy," began Mr. Cheney. "Read from the point in the scene — "

He was interrupted by a *thunk* from behind the curtain.

The Walking Disaster strikes again, I thought. But I was wrong. The *thunk* had been Alan Gray's elbow hitting the floor. Backstage, the pirates had grown bored, and Noodler and Smee had started another swordfight. Logan had backed Alan into a corner and hissed, "Walk the gangplank, traitor!" and Alan had lost his balance.

"Sorry!" called Logan.

Mr. Cheney closed his eyes briefly. When he had collected himself, he asked Kristy and me to begin reading.

Kristy read.

I changed my lines.

When the time came for me to sew on Peter's shadow, I said, "Oh, Peter, sewing is so simple. Here. Take this needle and thr — "

"Dawn," interrupted Mr. Cheney, "if you aren't sure of your lines, please use your script."

"Okay," I said.

We continued the scene. Mr. Cheney listened to us closely.

I tried to stick to the script, but soon I found myself saying, "Peter, I'll be happy to come to Neverland with you, and teach the Lost Boys how to cook. Then they can — "

Mr. Cheney interrupted again. "What are you doing, Dawn?"

"Well, *Peter Pan* is a little old-fashioned. Don't you think? It's awfully sexist."

"I think it's terrific!" called a male voice from backstage.

"Mr. Cheney, I'm just trying to update the story," I said.

"It's going to be difficult to improve on Sir James Barrie's lines, Dawn. Besides, we are putting on the traditional story."

"Oh, we can keep the fairies and the flying and everything."

"Thank you," said Mr. Cheney drily.

"No, really. We can do the traditional story. We'll just change some of the words so kids don't get any wrong ideas."

I heard a snicker then, and Cokie stepped out of the wings. She tried to say something, but she began to laugh and couldn't stop.

"Miss Mason?" said Mr. Cheney.

"I'm sorry. It's just . . . Dawn, I can't believe you want to change the play. And anyway, what wrong ideas are you talking about?"

"About women's roles. And men's. Really, when you think about it, we shouldn't refer to 'women's roles' and 'men's roles' at all. Both women and men can and should do everything."

"You like the idea of women fighting in wars?" asked Cokie.

"There shouldn't be wars in the first place," I said.

Cokie was still trying not to laugh. "But, Dawn — "

"Excuse me, girls," said Mr. Cheney. He was speaking with very tense lips, which is never a good sign. "We are supposed to be rehearsing. Cokie, you are not in this scene, so please go back to whatever you were doing. Dawn, say Mr. Barrie's lines as they're written. And Kristy, please do not refer to your script quite so much. At least look at Dawn when you're talking to her, not at the paper."

"Okay," said Kristy and Cokie and I.

Cokie disappeared behind the curtain, and Kristy and I returned to the scene we'd been rehearsing. We said about four more lines before Mr. Cheney called, "Dawn, please project! Kristy, quit looking at the script!"

"Okay," we replied.

Three more lines.

"Kristy! Script!"

"Sorry," said Kristy.

Five more lines.

"Dawn, project!"

From behind the curtain I heard Cokie giggling. Then I heard her say to someone, "Notice that Mr. Cheney never has to tell *Kristy* to project."

"Mr. Cheney," Kristy protested. "Did you hear Cokie?"

"Yes. Yes, I did." Mr. Cheney raised his voice for Cokie's benefit. "Cokie, please contain yourself," he said. Then he lowered his voice. "Okay, girls."

I started to say my next line, but instead I laid my script carefully on the stage. I walked over to Mr. Cheney and said, "Does Wendy *really* have to sew on Peter's shadow for him? Can't she give him the needle and thread — the pre*tend* needle and thread — and say, 'Peter, I won't sew it on for you, but I'll be happy to teach *you* how to sew it on'?"

"Peter doesn't have all night, Dawn!" called Cokie.

And Mr. Cheney, after sighing again, said, "Think of it this way. Peter is just a boy. He needs someone to help him."

"But Wendy is just a girl."

"She's a girl who knows how to sew," said Mr. Cheney.

"But Peter says he wants a *mother* for the Lost Boys."

By this time, Kristy had laid her script on the floor, too, and was standing next to me. "Give it a rest, Dawn," she said.

"Okay, okay, okay."

We returned to our scripts, but before we could pick them up, Mr. Cheney, smiling brightly, said, "How about if you try the rest of this scene without the scripts?" I think he was trying to distract us. (He looked as if he might have a headache.)

I pretended I had just sewn Peter's shadow back on him. I waited expectantly for Kristy to say her next line.

Kristy opened her mouth. Then she closed it.

I heard Cokie whisper loudly, "It's a miracle. Kristy Thomas is speechless."

"Mr. Cheney," complained Kristy.

"Cokie," complained Mr. Cheney.

I had a feeling we were all about to get in trouble. Instead, Logan got thrown out of the play.

CHAPTER 11

LOGAN

MONDAY

WHAT A MESS. OKAY, SO I DID SOME-
THING DISTRACTING. OKAY, WORSE THAN
DISTRACTING. OKAY, NOT EVEN VERY
SMART. BUT I DON'T THINK I DESERVED
TO GET THROWN OUT OF THE PLAY. AND
I DON'T THINK I WOULD HAVE BEEN
THROWN OUT OF THE PLAY IF DAWN
HADN'T CLIMBED UP ON HER WOMEN'S
MOVEMENT SOAPBOX, OR IF SHE AND
KRISTY AND COKIE HADN'T BUGGED
MR. CHENEY ALL AFTERNOON. IF IT HAD
BEEN A NORMAL REHEARSAL, I
WOULDN'T HAVE BEEN SO BORED, AND
MR. CHENEY WOULDN'T HAVE BEEN SO
FRUSTRATED.

Of all the pirates, I *would* have to be cast as that one guy named Noodler. The other pirates have some weird names, like Mr. Smee and Skylights, but most of them have more regular names — Bill Jukes, Alf Mason, Gentleman Starkey. How did I wind up as Noodler? At least I'm not playing a Lost Boy. One of the Lost Boys is named Tootles. Luckily, that part went to little Melody Korman, who can handle it. But think if *I* had to play a character named Tootles. I would have been laughed off the track team.

At first, I wouldn't even tell anyone about the Noodler business. When Mr. Cheney posted the cast for *Peter Pan*, I told my parents I'd gotten a role as a pirate which, it turns out, they already knew because Ms. Halliday had called our house that afternoon to tell us that Kerry, who had also auditioned, was going to be an Indian.

"Are you going to be Smee?" my father had asked me at dinner.

"No. Just some pirate," I told him.

But I couldn't keep my secret for long. Every kid who had looked at the chart that day had seen my name next to the name Noodler.

At least I got to *be* in the play. I figured I could deal with the name as long as I could be part of *Peter Pan*. It was important to me. Most of my friends were involved with the play. Pete Black was going to be Nana and the crocodile, although no one would know. (Those animal costumes are huge and you can't see who's inside them.) My girlfriend Mary Anne, who refused to be in the play, ended up working on it anyway. And a bunch of her friends (who are also my friends, since we're all in the Baby-sitters Club) were in the play. Plus, one is designing the scenery, another is working on the costumes, and another is choreographing dances for the little kids.

The point in all this is — Well, actually there are two points. 1) I desperately wanted to be in the play, and I got my chance when I was given the part of Noodler. 2) Since most of my friends were working on the play, they were all around to see Mr. Cheney fire me.

I've never been fired from anything before. I mean, not just out-and-out fired in front of a whole bunch of people.

Here's the problem. There wasn't a lot for the pirates to do just then. We didn't have many lines to learn, and we only appeared in two scenes. Two high-profile, highly important scenes, but still, just two scenes. The little kids (the Indians and Lost Boys) appear in more scenes, and anyway, it takes them longer to learn their parts and the musical numbers, so Jessi and Ms. Halliday are working with them practically nonstop.

What I'm trying to say is that the pirates had sort of been fooling around at rehearsals. No one seemed to need us, except Savannah Minton and Mallory Pike who had to measure us for our costumes. (Mallory was embarrassed out of her mind. She made me measure myself and read the numbers to her, and then she made this great show of writing down the numbers on a sheet of paper, like that was really all her job was — just recording numbers, not using the measuring tape.)

Well, I keep getting away from the point, which just goes to show you how embarrassed I am to tell how I was fired. Okay. So on Monday, which was, like, our third rehearsal or something, this is what was going on. Jessi and Ms. Halliday were teaching dances to the Lost Boys and the Indians. Mary Anne was helping Jackie Rodowsky learn his lines for the part of Michael Darling. Savannah and Mallory had finished measuring us pirates and were waiting to measure the little kids. The lighting people and set people and sound people were running around, figuring things out, making sketches, and taking notes. The kids with big roles and a lot of lines to memorize were rehearsing with each other or on the stage with Mr. Cheney.

And then there were us pirates. *We* had nothing to do.

We decided to have a swordfight. To our credit, we had realized we should practice swordfighting since pirates are always drawing out swords and having duels, and we wanted to look like authentic pirates. But our swordfighting was getting out of control.

On the other hand, we were having fun. Also, we were busy. And the more occupied we were, the less apt the other pirates were to remember I was playing a guy named Noodler.

After one lengthy duel in the wings off the stage, Alan Gray, who was playing Smee (and really should have been memorizing his lines), put down his sword (a twelve-inch ruler) and said, "Didn't Cheney say he might work with us pirates later this afternoon? If he isn't going to we might as well leave."

"I don't know. Did he say that?" I replied.

"I think he did," said the guy playing Gentleman Starkey.

I looked at my watch. "It's almost four-thirty."

"Cheney's all caught up with Dawn

Schafer," said Pete Black, who didn't have any more to do than the pirates did. He'd been listening to Dawn and Kristy who were rehearsing onstage, but now he joined us in the wings.

"What do you mean he's all caught up with Dawn?" I asked.

"Well, listen," Pete replied.

We moved closer to the curtain and listened. We could hear Dawn going on about women's lib or something. She was saying that Peter should sew on his own shadow and Wendy should give the Lost Boys cooking lessons.

"Is she crazy?" said Alan.

"She must be," I replied. "Give the Lost Boys *cook*ing lessons?"

"I don't mean that. I mean Cheney is going to kill her. If she's too much trouble he'll probably give the part of Wendy to Dawn's understudy."

We listened to the conversation awhile longer. Finally Pete said, "Cheney won't get around to working with you guys today. Not now. It's too late."

"Thanks to Dawn," said Alan. He put down his ruler and wandered among the kids backstage. I followed him.

"Hey!" I started to call to Mary Anne, but she was involved with Jackie Rodowsky. She was feeding him his lines and Jackie was repeating them, trying to memorize them. He kept mixing up words, saying them in the wrong order, and Mary Anne looked completely frustrated.

I decided it might be a good idea to try to amuse her. "Hey, Alan!" I called. "Come here!"

Earlier that afternoon, Alan and I had found a box containing parts of the pirate costumes. They were the parts that didn't have to be any particular size, like eye patches, earrings, scarves, and . . . plastic swords. Before I knew it, Alan and I and a couple of other guys, including Pete who wasn't even a pirate, were wearing these sort of half-pirate costumes, and dueling with the plastic swords.

Mary Anne ran over to us. "Logan!" she exclaimed. "What are you doing? Put that sword down!"

I stopped dueling with Alan, but I didn't put the sword down. Instead I raised it above my head, arm outstretched, and shouted, "Mutiny! The pirates are going to mutiny!"

Silence.

Uh-oh.

*Every*thing grew quiet. The kids faltered in their dancing and stood still. Sam and Stacey

110

stopped reading their scene aloud. Mallory and Savannah halted in their tracks and their tape measures fell to the floor. Onstage, the voices of Kristy, Dawn, and Mr. Cheney stopped speaking.

Everyone and everything was still for maybe four seconds. And then the curtain parted wildly and Mr. Cheney strode through it. He surveyed the scene. What he saw first was Alan and me in our pirate gear. What he saw second was everyone else looking at us.

"Logan! Alan!" roared Mr. Cheney.

"He started it," said Alan immediately, pointing to me.

"Traitor," I muttered.

"Logan, this is not the first time you've fooled around," said Mr. Cheney. "I've been watching you." Oh, fine. "Were you the one who just yelled 'mutiny'?"

"Yes, sir."

Mr. Cheney counted to ten before he spoke again. I know he did. I could see his lips moving. "Look around you, Logan. Do you see all these children?" Of course I saw them. "They are working. They are also looking up to you older kids. And you are not setting a very good example."

"No, sir."

"Logan, who is your understudy?"

"Jason Henderson. He's the understudy for me, Bill Jukes, and Gentleman Starkey."

"Fine. Jason is now Noodler. You're out of the play."

I stood rooted to the floor. I couldn't move. I had been fired.

CHAPTER 12

Kristy

Monday.

I think we would all like to forget today's rehearsal. And I, personally, would like to strangle Cokie Mason. She is such a pill. Okay, so Dawn is having a little trouble with the part of Wendy. And I'm having a little trouble memorizing my lines. (Who wouldn't? I have pages and pages of stuff to remember, plus about a billion songs to learn.) And Logan is having a little trouble in general. And so is Jackie. This does not make Cokie the Queen of the Play. But I guess she thinks it does.

The one good thing that came out of this afternoon is that Logan talked to Mr. Cheney when the rehearsal was over, and he's back in the play. But even that isn't so much good as it is not-bad. Logan shouldn't have gotten himself in a position to be fired from the play in the first place.

Logan definitely should not have been fooling around backstage today, having sword-fights and calling for mutinies. There's just no excuse for that kind of behavior. However, I was grateful to him for one reason. While Mr. Cheney was yelling at him, everyone forgot about Dawn and me and what was happening onstage.

I could not get over Dawn. What did she think she was doing? Wendy was supposed to fly to Neverland so she could teach the Lost Boys to *cook*? I understand Dawn's point. I'm a girl and I hate cooking and cleaning and sewing. And if I were Wendy Darling and some strange kid flew into my bedroom and asked me to go to a wonderful place like Neverland to do housework for a bunch of lost boys, I'd be furious. On the other hand, we had a play to put on, and I didn't think Dawn should contribute to the frazzled nerves of the director by changing the script without telling anyone in advance. No wonder I'm having trouble learning my lines. Dawn keeps changing hers. Still, Cokie didn't have to giggle every time Mr. Cheney called, "Kristy! Script!"

Oh, well. Then Logan yelled, "Mutiny!" and all was forgotten. Here's what happened after Mr. Cheney said to Logan, "You're out of the play."

The stunned silence that had fallen over the cast and crew of *Peter Pan* continued until Mr. Cheney clapped his hands twice and said gruffly, "Kristy and Dawn, you may rehearse on your own now. Cokie, I'd like to see you onstage by yourself, please." He turned to march back through the curtains, and Cokie, looking as stunned as the rest of us, followed him wordlessly. She didn't even give me a rude look.

"Whoa," I whispered to Dawn.

Around us, everyone came to life slowly. Ms. Halliday and Jessi began rehearsing the little kids again. Most of the older kids whispered to each other for a few moments, then returned to whatever they'd been doing before Mr. Cheney blew up. And Mary Anne left Jackie Rodowsky, took Logan by the elbow, and led him into the wings.

"Okay, let's get back to work," Dawn said to me briskly. "Let's start with the scene in the nursery, right before you're going to teach us Darling children how to fly."

"All right, but Dawn, *please* don't change any lines. No wonder I can't learn my own. I never know what you're going to say."

"I won't. I'll be good, I promise."

I smiled. "Thank you."

We began the scene. Dawn lived up to her promise. And I still couldn't say my lines unless I read them from the script.

"*Darn* it!" I cried.

"Relax, Kristy. You'll learn your lines."

"When?"

"This is only the third rehearsal."

"Well, you already know half your lines. And listen to Cokie out there with Mr. Cheney. She isn't using the script. And she's great."

"How do you know she isn't using the script?"

"Because I heard Mr. Cheney tell her to try working without it and she said okay. Now listen to her. Maybe Cokie should have been Peter Pan."

"Kristy! No wonder you haven't learned any lines. You're too busy paying attention to what everyone else is doing. Concentrate."

"I'm trying to."

"Try harder."

So I did. I guess by the end of rehearsal I was a *little* better.

117

Kristy

"Thank you, everybody," said Mr. Cheney at five-thirty. "Go home, work hard, and I'll see you back here on Wednesday."

My friends and I began to gather our things together. The backstage baby-sitter helped the little kids gather their things together. As the auditorium began to empty, I saw Logan appear from the wings. He parted the curtain and walked onto the stage, calling, "Mr. Cheney?"

Now, I did not mean to listen to their conversation. I really didn't. But Sam and David Michael and I were waiting for Charlie to pick us up, and he had said he was going to be late. And there was no way we were going to wait for him outside in the freezing cold any longer than necessary. So we were hanging around the auditorium.

By the way, in case you're wondering, the BSC had informed its clients that club meetings were going to be suspended during the rehearsals for *Peter Pan*, but that Claudia could take messages and arrange jobs (with over-the-phone help from Mary Anne) any time she was at home.

Anyway, Sam and a couple of his friends were talking backstage, and David Michael was hanging around them. And I was sitting

118

on the floor near the curtain, studying my lines, when I couldn't help but hear Logan say timidly, "Mr. Cheney?"

"Yes?" (Mr. Cheney's "yes" sounded pretty frosty.)

"Could I please talk to you?"

After a pause (maybe Mr. Cheney looked at his watch), he replied, "For a minute. I'm running late."

"Mr. Cheney, I would really like another chance to be in the play. Please. This is important to me. I know I haven't treated it as if it's important but it is. Could you give me another chance?"

"Do you think I should?"

"Yes, sir."

"Why?"

"Because I'm usually responsible. I don't know what got into me, but it won't happen again. And because you're usually fair," Logan added.

"All right. You are back in the play, Logan."

"Thanks!"

"But you are on probation. One more problem with you — if I so much as have to *think* about speaking to you like that again — and you really will be out of the play. Now could you please tell Jason Henderson I need to talk to him as soon as possible?"

"Sure," said Logan eagerly. "And thanks again. You won't be sorry."

Yes! I said to myself. All right, Logan! Good one!

I put down my script. I looked at my watch. Five more minutes until Charlie would arrive. Or maybe longer. I decided to get a drink of water. But no sooner had I stood up than I heard someone else onstage say, "Mr. Cheney?" The voice was not nearly as timid as Logan's had been.

It belonged to Cokie Mason.

"Hi, there," replied Mr. Cheney. "What's up?"

"I have to ask a favor."

(By this time I was eavesdropping shamelessly. No way was I going to leave for a drink of water.)

"Shoot," said Mr. Cheney.

"Well, I was wondering," began Cokie sweetly, "if later on I could have my own private dressing room."

Mr. Cheney coughed. "Your what?"

"My own dressing room."

"Cokie, no one has a dressing room."

"I know. But I've been watching all these little kids, and, well, backstage gets sort of zoo — I mean, crowded. Everyone is running around and everything, and I just don't know how I'm going to be able to put on my makeup when the time comes, and do it well. I'll need peace and quiet."

Oh, my lord! What an incredible prima donna. I held my breath, so as not to miss a word of Mr. Cheney's response.

"I'll see what I can do, but don't count on anything. As I said, *no* one has an actual dressing room. But later on, if you really think this is going to be a problem, maybe we can find someplace other than backstage where you can get ready for dress rehearsals and performances."

Brother. Cokie had practically gotten her way again. I stalked off for the water fountain after all. And on my way back to the auditorium I had another one of those brainstorms for which I'm becoming famous.

I ran backstage, hoping Cokie would still be around, and there she was. "Hey, Cokie!" I called. "Cokie, come here!"

Cokie looked at me suspiciously. "What?"

"Well, I didn't mean to eavesdrop," I said, "but I'm waiting around for my brother to pick me up and I heard you ask Mr. Cheney about a dressing room. I couldn't help it. Anyway, I have an idea. I thought of the *per*fect dressing room for you. In fact, I don't know why Mr.

Cheney didn't think of this. Want to see it?"

"Kristy, why are you being nice to me?" asked Cokie.

Good question. Cokie had been mean to me all afternoon, and we both knew it. Furthermore, we don't like each other anyway. I thought fast. "I'm not being nice to you. I was just thinking. If you really *are* going to have trouble with your makeup with all the kids around and all the noise, then you should have your own dressing room. We have to do the 'Ugg-a-Wugg' song, and I don't want you looking bad when we're onstage together. Besides, I want you out of my hair."

"Well, at least you're honest," said Cokie. "Okay. Where is this place?"

"Out in the hall. Come on."

I led Cokie into the hallway.

I led her straight to a mop closet.

"Here you go," I said.

"Kristy Thomas . . . you are a cretin," was Cokie's reply.

"Thank you," I said. I started laughing and couldn't stop.

Cokie got all huffy and walked away.

That night, I telephoned every single one of my friends and told them what I'd done. They were proud of me.

* * *

Two days later I was on my way to the next rehearsal and I passed the mop closet. A gold star had been stuck on the door.

I paused, gaping, and the door opened and Cokie came out. When she saw me, she grinned. "It's all mine," she said, and I knew she meant the closet. "Mr. Halprin said I could use it." (Mr. Halprin is the SMS janitor.)

I vowed revenge on Cokie Mason.

Jackie

Wensday

I never kept a dairy before. I hope I am writting what Jessi Ramsey wants. She said write about what hapens to me in the play. I will write about being Michal Darling and flying and those animal costums. And also Mary Ann she is my very speshul helper.

signed by Jackie Rodowsky

I feel like I have been Michael Darling for most of my life. We have been rehearsing and rehearsing and rehearsing. Mr. Cheney says we are being professionals because this isn't just some little class play. It is a production, a musical with costumes. And we are going to give several performances, including two at night. And people all over our town are going to *pay* to see the play. I have been to a few plays in Stamford, so I know this is a big deal. I understand why we have to rehearse so much.

The first rehearsals did not feel like rehearsals at all. I told Mary Anne so. She said, "Be patient, Jackie." And I tried to be.

Now the rehearsals are more like what I expected. When we rehearse a scene, everyone in that scene is onstage at the same time. And no one is allowed to read from the scripts anymore. We hardly ever say the whole scene from beginning to end, though. Mr. Cheney is always calling out, "Stop! Try that line again!" Or, "Wait! Go back to Peter Pan's last line!" Or, "Okay, here's where the musical number begins."

I do not mind that too much.

This is what I do mind: I do not get to fly. No one does. Not even Peter Pan. "It is too dangerous," Mr. Cheney said. "We will have to simulate flying." He uses that word "simulate" a lot. He says Karen Brewer has to simulate being a fairy, too.

How boring. When Mom and Dad took my brothers and me to see *Peter Pan*, Peter and Wendy and Michael and John got to fly all above the stage. I could kind of see the wires and of course I knew they were not really flying, but so what? And how come flying wasn't dangerous for them, but Mr. Cheney says it's dangerous for us? Grown-ups worry too much. Also, they are no fun.

This is how we are supposed to simulate flying: run across the stage with our arms outstretched, crying, "I'm flyyyyy-ing!"

I'm sure I can think of a better way. Maybe when we have our costumes.

We still do not have our costumes. Just pieces of them, like the pirates' eyepatches and John's tall silk hat. I don't care too much. My costume is a nightshirt, and I bet my friends will laugh when they see me in it. It looks more like a nightgown than a nightshirt. A *girl's* nightgown. So does John's nightshirt, but then he gets to wear that hat, and carry a black umbrella. Like a man. So I do not think kids will laugh at him.

Anyway, even though we cannot fly over

the stage, and even though my costume looks like a nightgown, I am still having fun playing Michael Darling. My brothers and I have always thought we should be in show business. Mary Anne Spier has been helping me with my part. She is a good helper. She is a good baby-sitter, too. She only did one thing wrong. She never told me about the crocodile. And that is what led to the trouble.

"Hi, Jackie!" called Mary Anne. "Ready to work?"

At each rehearsal, Mary Anne first helps all the little kids backstage. She has to since she's the backstage baby-sitter. Then when everyone is doing whatever they are supposed to do during the rehearsal, Mary Anne calls to me, and we work together. We are a team.

"Ready!" I called back.

"Mr. Cheney is running through Act One today," Mary Anne told me. "And I have a surprise for you."

"A surprise? What is it?"

"The costumes are here. Mallory just told me. She said Mr. Cheney's going to stop the rehearsal a little early today so everyone can try on the costumes. We have to be sure they fit. If they don't there's plenty of time to fix them. Okay, you're due onstage now. Remember, I'll be watching you from the wings most of the time. And if I'm not in the wings then I'll be nearby. Always let me know if you need anything."

"Thanks, Mary Anne," I said.

Mary Anne worries way too much, but I am glad she is my coach.

Mr. Cheney gathered together me and Dawn and Kristy and everyone who is in Act I. "Beginning to end," he told us. "Musical numbers, too."

I have to pay attention a *lot* when I am acting. I do not have as many lines to say as Kristy and Dawn do, but I am always supposed to be *do*ing a certain thing in a certain place while I am on the stage, so I cannot daydream while the other characters are speaking.

This is my favorite part of Scene One in Act I (and by the way, there is *only* one scene in Act I, so I do not know why they bother to *call* it Scene One, since there are no *other* scenes): Wendy and John and I are lying in our beds in the nursery, waiting for Peter Pan to come. Well, not *wait*ing, because in the play we do not know he's coming, but in real life we do. Anyway, once Kristy comes — I mean, once Peter Pan comes — then the flying begins. Peter teaches us to fly while we're singing "I'm Flying." This is after we have woken up and gotten out of our beds, of course. But we are still in the nursery. Peter keeps telling us to "think lovely thoughts." When we are thinking lovely enough thoughts, then we can fly. (But we also need to have a little pixie dust sprinkled on us.)

"Think lovely thoughts! Think lovely thoughts!" Peter Pan calls to us. And Tinker Bell, who is Karen Brewer, throws around some glitter.

We think our lovely thoughts. Wendy flies first, then John, then me.

"I'm flyyyyy-ing!" we yell as we run across the stage.

On that afternoon, I watched Kristy and Dawn and Barry Soeder run back and forth, their arms spread open. (Barry Soeder plays John. I do not know him at all. I mean, I didn't before the play. He goes to Stoneybrook Middle School with Mary Anne and everyone.)

"Think lovelier thoughts, Michael!" Peter Pan called to me, since I was the only one who still could not fly.

Just as Kristy said that line, I got a really good idea. I stood up on my bed. Then I climbed onto a dresser. Then I climbed onto this very tall box that happened to be standing right behind the dresser. Something had been delivered in that box earlier in the day. The box wouldn't be around when we were performing the play for real, but I'd figure out something else then. For now, I bent my knees and got ready to jump.

Mr. Cheney raced across the stage and caught me just before I was airborne. He set me down. "Jackie, what on earth were you doing?"

"I was going to fly. It would have looked very realistic."

"You would have broken your neck. You were going to jump onto a hard floor from six feet up. Don't ever do that again!"

"I'm sorry."

"All right, start over from your last line, Kristy," said Mr. Cheney.

"Um . . . I can't just start in the middle like that. Where's my script?" said Kristy. She looked offstage.

"You should know your lines by now," said Mr. Cheney.

"Mr. Cheney? Can't we *please* have flying ropes?" I asked.

"No."

"How about if I just jump off the dresser?"

"No."

"I want flying ropes, too, Mr. Cheney," said

Karen Brewer. "Tinker Bell has to fly, you know. All fairies fly."

"NO FLYING ROPES!" yelled Mr. Cheney.

"Okay," we replied.

I decided I would practice jumping off of my own dresser at home.

We finally made it to the end of Act I, and when we did, Mr. Cheney wiped his forehead with a handkerchief. Then he took a couple of aspirins. After that he said he needed a little rest. So he sat down in the auditorium and Miss Stanworth came on the stage. Miss Stanworth is the head costume lady. She called to the cast and everyone crowded onto the stage.

"Your costumes are here," she announced. "I would like you to try them on, and I personally want to look at each one of you in your costume before you leave today. Savannah and Mallory will help you."

I ran to Mary Anne. "How did I do?" I asked her.

"Fine, until you nearly killed yourself. Come on. Let's get your costume."

Backstage, Savannah and Mallory were calling out names and handing each kid a pile of clothes.

"Jackie Rodowsky!" call Savannah, and I ran to her.

She handed me a white nightshirt. Sure enough, it looked exactly like this nightgown my mom wears.

I sighed. I sulked.

Mary Anne made me put it on anyway.

The boys were changing in the wings off stage right. The girls were changing in the wings off stage left. Everyone who wanted to see how we looked was waiting for us in the middle.

I stepped out of the wings.

"Terrific!" exclaimed Mary Anne when she saw me. "You look just — "

"Like my mother?" I suggested.

"No, like Michael Darling."

"Oh. Okay. Can I go take this — Aughhh!" I screamed. "Aughhh!"

I ran for cover. I hid behind a piece of scenery Claudia was painting.

"Jackie, what's wrong?" cried Mary Anne when she found me.

"I saw a monster! Didn't you see him?"

"A monster? Jackie — "

"Aughhh! There he is again!"

Mary Anne turned around. She smiled. "Jackie, that's Pete Black. That's the crocodile costume. Pete plays Nana and the crocodile, remember?"

132

"Yes."

No matter who was in that costume, I didn't like it. It was scary.

The second time I saw that crocodile was at our next rehearsal. We were running through Act II. We were wearing our costumes. The crocodile wiggled and slithered out of the wings. I turned around and he was right behind me. I could see all of his teeth.

"Aughhh!" I screamed.

I stepped backward.

CRASH!

I fell off the stage. (I landed on a pile of coats.)

"Jackie," Mary Anne said to me later. "Are you still afraid of the croc?"

"Yes," I admitted.

"But he's going to be onstage with you from now on."

Uh-oh.

CHAPTER 14

Jessi

Friday

I have to help everyone. Everyone. I don't know how this play would get produced without me. Kristy doesn't know her lines yet. We've all been coaching her. And she still forgets. Mallory is always asking me for costuming advice. And of course, there's my work with the little kids. My choreography. Now

I see the real reason Mr. Cheney didn't cast me as Peter Pan. He needed an assistant producer. But if that's true, then explain to me what happened when the kid from the print shop came to rehearsal today with the copy for the play program. Doesn't anyone appreciate me?

I stood before a row of little kids. Nicky Pike, Myriah Perkins, David Michael Thomas, and Bill and Melody Korman. Four of the kids were dancing. Nicky was standing still in the center of the row.

"Okay, hold it, you guys!" I said. "Nicky, what's wrong?"

"I feel like a ballerina. I am not dancing in tights."

"Nicky, you've had your costume for a week now," I pointed out.

Nicky shrugged. Then he said, "I saw *Peter Pan* on TV. The Lost Boys were not wearing tights."

"Maybe they weren't performing in the middle of winter," I said. "Miss Stanworth added tights to your costumes so you won't freeze to death. It's fourteen degrees outside."

"And it doesn't feel much warmer in here," called Dawn from nearby.

"Anyway, boy ballet dancers wear tights," I said. "And they aren't called ballerinas. They're just dancers." Nicky scowled. "Take it from the top, kids!" I called. "You, too, Nicky."

The Lost Boys started over again.

From onstage, I heard Mr. Cheney say, "Check your script, Kristy."

We had been rehearsing forever. Well, *I* hadn't been, since I'm not in the play, but you know what I mean. Anyway, we were now rehearsing in our costumes (most of the time) and opening night was just a couple of weeks away. I wondered if Mr. Cheney was getting tired of telling Kristy to check her script all the time. I wondered if he was getting *nervous* because he still had to do that. I wondered if he wished he had cast somebody else in the role of Peter Pan.

"Oh, Mrs. Darling! Mrs. Darling!"

Sam Thomas was running around backstage, looking for Stacey. He never called her Stacey anymore.

"Yeah?" replied Stace. She stepped away from a bunch of our friends.

"I can't tie my tie, Mother," said Sam, looking pathetic. (In the play, Mrs. Darling spends a good deal of time helping Mr. Darling with his tie.)

Stacey's face turned red. She tried to smile at Sam, but she didn't say anything. I don't think she knew what to say.

I turned back to the Lost Boys. I turned back in time to watch David Michael. "Okay," I said, "now step, step, cross-step, careful, careful — "

Thud.

David Michael cross-stepped, lost his balance, and sat down on his bottom. He did that absolutely every time we reached this particular point in the dance routine.

"BULLFROGS!" cried David Michael, with full lung power.

"It's all right. Try again," I said.

"But we're *tired*, Jessi," whined Nicky.

"Okay. Take a break." I raised my voice. "Indians, get ready to dance!"

The Indians surrounded me. Before I could organize them, Kerry Bruno stepped over to me. "Jessi, Jessi," she whispered urgently.

"What is it?" I asked. I led her away from the group.

Kerry stood on tiptoe, and I leaned over. She whispered to me, between cupped hands, "I want to be an Indian maiden."

"You are an Indian maiden," I whispered back.

"But I want to look like Tiger Lily. I just decided that. Tiger Lily is glamorous. The other Indians aren't."

"Tiger Lily is special," I told her. "Only Tiger Lily can look like Tiger Lily. Besides, she's supposed to be an Indian *princess*."

"I want to be an Indian princess."

"I think you'll have to talk to Mr. Cheney about that."

"Then I'm telling Logan!"

Out of nowhere Logan appeared. "Telling me what?" he said.

"That I want to be an Indian princess like Tiger Lily."

"And I told her she'd have to talk to Mr. Cheney," I said.

"Oh, Kerry, please don't do that," Logan pleaded. "The Bruno family has caused enough trouble already. Besides, I know what Cheney will say when you tell him you want to be an Indian princess."

"What will he say?"

"He'll say no. So there's no point in asking."

"Well . . . well . . ." Kerry glanced at David Michael. "Well, bullfrogs!"

Logan grinned. "You're a regular old Indian, sis. You better get used to it."

The rehearsal continued. It was almost over when Mr. Cheney said, "May I have your attention, please? Will everyone gather onstage? Crew, too."

Now this was interesting. What kind of announcement was Mr. Cheney going to make? Maybe he had decided on a small change in the cast. A change involving Kristy and me . . . . No, he probably wouldn't haul off and formally announce something like that. More likely he would take the two of us aside. Then, privately, he would break the news.

"Kristy," he would say, "I've been working with you for several weeks now and, well, simply put, you are not learing your lines fast enough. I'm getting worried about opening night. I'm not sure you'll be prepared. So I've decided to replace you."

"With my understudy?" Kristy would ask.

"No, with Jessi Ramsey, the person I should have cast as Peter Pan in the first place. Kristy, please turn in your costume."

Compared to the dialogue I was imagining,

Jessi

Mr. Cheney's announcement was fairly tame. But it was interesting.

"The students in the print shop," he said, "are getting ready to go to press with the programs for the play. They want to make sure no one's name is missing from the program, that your names are spelled correctly, and that your proper role or title follows your name. Every member of both the cast and the crew should be included. Please check the list before you leave today and make any corrections. Younger kids, ask for help if you need it. And if you can think of anyone who isn't here this afternoon, please let me know. Thank you."

The list was on a desk at one side of the stage. Within seconds, everyone had surged around it. Ms. Halliday put an end to the madhouse by organizing us into a line. I was somewhere in the middle of the line. Just in front of me was Kerry Bruno.

When we reached the table, Kerry leaned over to peer at the list. She stamped her foot angrily. Then she turned to me and whispered, "Jessi, after my name it says 'Indian.' Could I change that to 'Indian Princess?' "

I shook my head. "Sorry, Kerry. Besides, the list will be checked later. Mr. Cheney or someone would just change it back."

"Bullfrogs," said Kerry, but I don't think she was *too* upset.

When Kerry left, I ran my finger down the list to the R names. I saw:

JESSICA RAMSEY: Assistant Choreographer

Assistant Choreographer? Was that all Mr. Cheney thought I did? Hadn't he seen me coaching some of the kids? Hadn't he seen Mallory asking me for advice? I came to each and every rehearsal, and I worked *hard*. (Not to mention that I should have been Peter Pan, in which case I would have worked even harder. And I would have known my lines by now.)

For a moment I hesitated over the list. Then I left it, and walked backstage. I sat on a plastic milk crate. I considered my options. I could change my credit — but I had just told Kerry not to change hers. I could talk to Mr. Cheney.

Or I could cross my name off the list.

I stood up slowly and returned to the desk on the stage. Four people were still standing in line. Everyone else had gone home. The auditorium was silent. And except for the five of us onstage, it was empty. When the other kids had checked the list and were putting on their coats, I stood by the desk. I looked at my name again. Then I removed a pen from my purse and drew a single heavy line through my name and my credit.

I put the pen back.

When I turned around, Mr. Cheney was standing behind me. "Why did you do that?" he asked quietly.

"Because — Because — " Suddenly I just couldn't think of a single thing to say. For weeks I'd been imagining scenes, confrontations, between Mr. Cheney and me. Now nothing I had planned to say sounded quite right.

"I do understand that you wanted to be Peter Pan," said Mr. Cheney gently. "You may not think so, but I do. However, I explained to you why I gave the part to a less experienced student. Also, Jessi, your dancing ability and your stage presence are phenomenal. But your singing and acting are, well . . . you don't have much more experience in those areas than Kristy does. Anyway, I appreciate how helpful you've been at rehearsals. Everyone has been helpful, really, but you're working wonders with the younger children. I'm glad you're associated with the production."

"Thank you," I mumbled.

Mr. Cheney hadn't said anything about crediting me as assistant producer. Maybe I didn't deserve it. I had no idea. What I did know now was that there was not a chance, not a single chance, I would somehow wind up as Peter Pan. Yet Mr. Cheney seemed glad I was working on the play. Feeling totally confused, I walked out of the auditorium.

CHAPTER 15

Stacey

Friday

Opening night is one week away.
Just one little week. Seven measly
days. I do not think we are going to
be ready for it. The show will have
to go on, of course. But I can just
imagine it. Props will fall, and kids
will run onstage when they're not
supposed to, and the Lost Boys will
sing the wrong words to the "Wendy"
song because Dawn has been trying
to change it, and Kristy will forget
a line and the audience will hear a
big gap of nothing, and then Jackie
will try to fly off the dresser....

Maybe I was just a teeny bit panicky, but *really*. A week until opening night and all these mistakes. Or could it be that I was concentrating on everyone else so I wouldn't have to concentrate on Sam and me? Am I making any sense? Let me explain things by describing a typical rehearsal, the Friday afternoon rehearsal. Then you'll see what I mean.

Mr. Cheney planned for us to run through the play from beginning to end in our costumes. But we were not holding an actual dress rehearsal, since we were not bothering with makeup, and since Mr. Cheney had told us he was going to feel free to interrupt us at any given moment.

So the play began. The Darling children are the first people on the stage. They are playing in their nursery, and it is very early in the evening. In the story, Sam and I, who are the Darling parents of the Darling children, are getting ready to go out to dinner. I am dressed in a long, lovely white evening gown, and Mr. Darling is also dressed formally, except that he has not yet tied his tie.

When Sam and I are onstage, we call each other Mother and Father. Or I call him Father dear and he calls me dearest. Things like that. It is a good thing I'll be wearing a lot of makeup during the performances, because every time I have to call Sam "Father," I blush terribly.

Sam, however, does not blush back.

Furthermore, guess what he calls me when we are *not* onstage. He calls me Mrs. Darling, Mother, and dearest. When he telephones me at home he says to Mom, "Is Mrs. Darling there, Mrs. McGill?" When he wants to get my attention during a rehearsal, he yells from the wings, "Hey, Mother! Mother, my darling, my dear!"

My cheeks are permanently red.

On Friday, while the Darling children and Nana were onstage, Sam and I, all dressed up, waited in the wings to make our entrance.

"Mother, you look divine," said Sam. He thought for a moment. Then he added, "Mrs. Darling, you look darling." He burst out laughing.

Oh, wonderful. I was performing with Jerry Lewis. Worse, I was going *out* with Jerry Lewis. I smiled weakly at Sam.

Sam glanced around, caught sight of a couple of his friends from the high school, and threw his arm around my shoulders. He was being playful.

"Stop!" I hissed. "We have to listen for our cues."

Moments later we were onstage with our Darling children and Nana. I was supposed to help Sam tie his tie. (Frankly, I've never understood why men can't do that themselves. They can tie their shoes, can't they?) I was standing so close to him we were almost embracing.

I heard a giggle.

I don't think Mr. Cheney heard it. If he had, he would have stopped the rehearsal. He absolutely expects us to act mature and responsible. When we don't, he calls us on it. (To be perfectly honest, he has been much worse about this ever since Logan yelled, "Mutiny!")

The giggle had come from Cokie. I couldn't look around to see where she was, since the script did not read *Mrs. Darling checks around the stage to see who's making fun of her*, but I was sure she was nearby, probably in the wings.

I was wrong. She was sitting in the front row of the auditorium, dressed as Tiger Lily. Grace Blume was next to her. I caught sight of them as I began the "Tender Shepherd" number with Dawn and Jackie and Barry Soeder. Which is another thing. Dawn and I can sing okay, but we are not exactly professionals. Sometimes our voices fade away. When they do, Mr. Cheney yells, "Sing out, Louise!" which apparently is a line from something, only no one knows what, except for Ms. Halliday who always grins while Dawn and I get flustered and then try both to compose ourselves *and* to sing out.

So here is the scene. Mr. Darling had left the stage, much to my relief, and much to the amusement of Cokie and Grace, although I don't know why they thought that was funny. Maybe Sam was doing some Jerry Lewis thing that Mr. Cheney and I missed. I was onstage with my children, and we were performing "Tender Shepherd."

". . . let me help you count your sheep," we sang.

"Sing out, Louise!" called Mr. Cheney, meaning Dawn and me.

We raised our voices. "One in the meadow, two in the garden . . ."

Finally the song ended and I made my exit.

"Lovely, my darling Mrs. Darling," Sam greeted me backstage.

I gave him another of my weak smiles.

"Yo, Sam!" called his friend Brian (softly enough so Mr. Cheney wouldn't hear).

In a flash, Sam's arm was around my waist. "Brian. Mr. Durang," he said heartily. "Have you met my mother? I mean, my wife?"

Brian extended his hand toward me. "I don't

believe I've had the pleasure, Mrs. . . . um
. . ." He pretended to look embarrassed.

"Darling," Sam supplied.

"Excuse me?" said Brian.

By now, this was an old, old routine. Sam
could not stop playing with our names. "Mrs.
Darling," repeated Sam. "Mother."

"Your mother?"

"My dearest dar — "

I tried to extricate myself from Sam. "Excuse
me," I said. "Sam?"

"Yes, dearest?"

"Let's see what's happening onstage. Kristy
has made her entrance."

"Okay." Sam tore himself away from Brian.
We edged closer to the stage. Peter Pan was
in the darkened Darling nursery talking to
Wendy. Michael and John were pretending to
be asleep in their beds. Wendy was preparing
to sew Peter's shadow onto his feet.

"I daresay it will hurt a little," she said.

"Oh, I shan't cry," Peter replied.

Dawn pretended to sew on the shadow.
Then she stepped back to admire her work.
She frowned. "Perhaps I should have ironed
it. . . . I mean, perhaps I should have shown
you how to iron it."

"Stop!" yelled Mr. Cheney. "Dawn
Schafer — "

"Sorry, sorry." Dawn repeated the line correctly.

Peter Pan began to jump gleefully around the stage, as if he had sewn on the shadow by himself. "How clever I am!" cried Kristy.

This was followed by silence.

Dawn and Kristy looked expectantly at each other.

"Your line," Kristy said to Dawn, as if they were playing chess, and Dawn had lost track of whose turn it was.

"Not until you finish your line," replied Dawn.

"Uh-oh," said Kristy.

Karen, in her Tinker Bell costume, leaped gracefully off the windowsill where she had been perched during this part of the scene. She tossed a handful of silver glitter in the air and cried, "Tinker Bell to the rescue! Your next line is, 'Oh, the cleverness of me!' Kristy."

"Stop!" yelled Mr. Cheney again. "Karen, thank you for trying to help, but you may *not* do that during a performance. You know that, don't you?" Mr. Cheney was massaging his temples, his eyes closed.

"Yes," said Karen contritely. She retreated to the windowsill.

The first act continued without incident.

Act II began.

Sam and I were not in Act II. We relaxed backstage. We watched Mallory and Savannah help Pete into the crocodile costume. The costume was spectacular. That's the only word for it. It was a green suit, which Pete got into standing up, but then lay in on the floor, stomach facing down, arms and legs extended. The crocodile's back, and the tops of his legs and tail were sequined. His stomach and the undersides of his legs and tail were felt, to help him slide across the stage. Pete had perfected his slither and could scoot across the stage crocodile-style, looking quite realistic, and moving fast when necessary. In order to see, he peered out through the croc's gaping jaws with its rows of plastic teeth.

When Pete had been zipped into the costume, he sprawled onto his stomach and waited in the wings for his cue to slither onstage.

Sam and I watched him go.

Several seconds later we heard a scream. It was followed by a scuffle.

Jackie Rodowsky flew into the wings where Mary Anne caught him.

"Save me!" he screeched.

Sam watched this calmly. Then he turned toward me, looked at me tenderly, and said, "There seems to be some sort of problem with our youngest child, my dearest darling Mrs. Darling."

Suddenly I had had it. Maybe Kristy had been right all along. Maybe her brother was nothing but a jerk. I stepped away from him. "Cut it *out*," I whispered loudly.

Sam looked at me, shocked and hurt. "What did I do?"

"Nothing. Leave me alone." I stalked off. I needed a place to sulk.

CHAPTER 16

Sam

Friday

Women. Who needs them? Who
can understand them? Unfortunately
the sad truth is, I need them. But
I don't think I'll ever understand
them. Sometimes my own grandmother
gets fed up with me. And Kristy
is always flying off the handle
whenever I say the littlest thing
to her, especially if it concerns her
appearance. And when I make a
goof call during one of her BSC
meetings... well, now she usually
just hangs up on me. But anyway,
today I don't know what I did to
make Stacey hiss at me and then
turn her back and go marching off.
   Oh. I just remembered I'm
supposed to be writing about the

*progress of the play, not my poor
relationships with women. So. The
play is fine.
Now if I could just figure out
Stacey. If she would just talk to
me like a human being ....*

Stacey McGill is terrific. She really is. She's gorgeous and sophisticated and funny and smart and popular. I've liked her for a long time. Over the summer, when I finally got around to telling her that, she said (at first) that basically she thought I was a jerk. That was understandable. Kristy has brainwashed all of her friends into thinking just that. Then Stacey confessed that when she first moved here, when she was in seventh grade, she had a crush on me.

I guess our timing was a little off.

"Get it together, Sam," Charlie said to me.

We got it together. We've been going out for awhile now, mostly to movies, or hanging around Stacey's house. Stacey keeps asking why she can't meet more of my friends. She wants to do other things, like go to school dances or parties. But I'm having a little problem with that. The problem is that I go to the high school and Stacey goes to the middle school. I'm in tenth grade and Stacey is in eighth.

My friends call me a cradle-robber.

They refer to Stacey as my "grade-school girlfriend."

And they say things like, "What time does she have to go down for her nap?" "Do you have to get a permission slip from her mommy before you can take her out?" "Are you going to take her to dinner or just give her a bottle?" They think these things are hysterical.

Stacey would die if she knew what my friends said. So I've been trying to keep them apart.

Then came the play and, as I heard some actor say once, our worlds collided. I guess that's a little strong. What I mean is, I could no longer file Stacey in one part of my life, and my friends in another. They had been brought together naturally.

I guess I didn't *have* to try out for the play. If I hadn't, then nobody would have seen Stacey and me together. But I *wanted* to be in the play. And I'll tell you the truth: I think I also kind of wanted people to see Stacey and me. I was tired of playing "keepaway" with her. I was tired of hiding out.

I did not, however, expect that Stacey and I would wind up as Mr. and Mrs. Darling. I know Stacey was embarrassed by that. Well, guess what. So was I. But I figured there must be some way to overcome the situation.

I decided to talk to Charlie.

Now, Charlie is not exactly Mr. Stud. He is not the Dating God. But he is my brother and he's two years older than me and he has had several girlfriends. So I asked him for advice.

"Do you and Stacey have fun when you're together?" Charlie wanted to know.

"Sure."

"As much fun as you'd have if she were a couple years older?"

"Yeah, I guess."

"So just let your friends know that."

"What do you mean?"

"When you and Stacey are together — at rehearsals or whatever — show everyone how much fun you're having." Charlie shrugged, as if to say, "Why couldn't *you* have thought of that?"

"Oh. All right."

So that's what I'd been doing. I was making a big joke out of the Mr. and Mrs. Darling thing. I was practically screaming out, "See? See how much fun my grade-school girlfriend and I are having?"

Only Stacey never seemed to be having quite as much fun as I was pretending we were having. I would approach her, grinning, and say something like, "Good evening, my dearest Mother." And Stacey would just sort of smile awkwardly at me.

But she had never backed away and told me to leave her alone. How was I supposed to react to that? At first, I did leave her alone. But by Act III we had to appear onstage again together. And since, as far as I know, Mr. and Mrs. Darling have not had a fight during Act II, we had to be civil with each other. More accurately, we had to appear happy. After all, our children had come home from Neverland and besides, we love each other.

Stacey and I made it through the rehearsal with gritted teeth — when we were together. The rest of the time we steered clear of each other. But I kept my eye on Stacey.

I watched her and Mary Anne try to calm down Jackie Rodowsky.

"I turned around and that crocodile was right behind me!" said Jackie, gasping. "He looks like a monster."

"But he isn't," Mary Anne replied gently. "You have to remember that."

"Yeah. It's just a costume, a *croc*odile costume, and Pete Black is inside," added Stacey. "You know Pete. He's inside the Nana costume, too."

"I know, I know. But when I see him and I'm not expecting him, he scares me," said Jackie, sounding frustrated.

"Well, the show must go on," said Stacey. "I hate to say this, Jackie, but you can't be afraid of the croc *and* be in the play. Because you absolutely cannot go screaming off the stage on opening night the moment the crocodile appears. I know I sound mean, but this is true. Mr. Cheney isn't going to allow it much longer."

Jackie turned to Mary Anne, I guess because she's usually pretty easy on the little kids. She smiled at him. "Stacey's right, Jackie."

Jackie sighed. "If only the crocodile weren't so sneaky."

Stacey and Mary Anne exchanged worried glances, and I knew why. Just one week until opening night. Sheesh.

Jackie watched Pete slip in and out of both the crocodile costume and the Nana costume after rehearsal a couple of times. Mary Anne thought this would be therapy for him. I watched the other kids hang up their costumes, watched Savannah and Mallory check them, watched Mr. Cheney talk to Karen about something . . . and waited for Stacey.

When I saw her, already wearing her coat, hurrying toward the hallway, I ran to her, caught her arm, and said, "Hey, Stace. We have to talk."

"I know."

"Where can we go?"

"Nowhere now. My mom's waiting for me."

"Tomorrow morning? Before rehearsal?"

"Okay."

"I'll meet you at Renwick's at ten. Is that all right? For breakfast or tea or soda or whatever you want."

"That's perfect," Stacey replied.

In Renwick's we sat at a booth. We looked at the menu quickly, and placed our orders. Stacey regarded me seriously.

"I was surprised you wanted to meet me in public," she said.

"That's mean, Stacey."

"And I'm surprised you're calling me Stacey. I thought you'd forgotten my name. What happened to dearest and Mrs. Darling?"

"That's mean, too."

"I'm sorry. I know it was mean. But, Sam, *really*."

"Look, before you say anything else, let me explain a couple of things. I love going out with you, Stacey — "

"Are you breaking up with me?" she asked, alarmed.

"No! Just let me say this. I love going out with you, but the guys — *some* of the guys — at school have been giving me a hard time. They call me a cradle-robber, and make jokes because you still go to SMS."

"I didn't know that."

"I didn't want you to know it. I thought your feelings would be hurt. I also didn't want to stop going out with you. I like you too much. But I like my friends, too. I don't want to lose you *or* them."

"Do you really think you'll have to make that choice?" asked Stacey. "Do you think if you and I hung around together more your friends would say, 'Later, Sam'?"

I shrugged. "I was hoping not to find out. Anyway, Charlie said I should just show everyone what a fantastic time you and I have together."

"Sam!" exclaimed Stacey. "Is *that* why you've been fooling around so much, calling me those ridiculous names?"

"I guess."

Stacey closed her eyes briefly. She looked like Mr. Cheney in a moment of near defeat when he needs to regain his composure. "Sam," she said again, "if those guys are *really* your friends, they won't care if we go out. They might tease you a little, but they'll still be your friends." The waiter set our food on the table then. "Now eat up, Mr. Darling," she added. "And when we get to school today, just act like a normal human, and I'll do the same."

CHAPTER 17

Mary Anne

Monday

Countdown. Four days until opening night. I'm beginning to think we might — just might — be ready for it. I see a glimmer of hope. Jackie no longer runs (or falls) off the stage when he sees the crocodile. He just sort of yelps. When he does, Mr. Cheney looks at him strangely, but I've convinced him Jackie will have even the yelping under control by Friday. (I hope I'm right.)

Mary Anne

Unfortunately, we
have a small new
problem. Karen Brewer
recently saw Peter Pan
again. I think Kristy
rented it for her, and
I wish she hadnt.
Because now Karen
wants those sound
effects you hear whenever
Tinker Bell is around.
And no one has rehearsed
any Tink sound effects
since we have a real
live fairy. Mr. Cheney
says its too late to add
that "dimension" to
the play, and Karen is
not happy.
And... I guess there
is one other tiny little
problem. It's between
Mal and me. I wasn't
going to write about it,
but maybe I should.

I think the reason behind Mallory's problem was something she didn't want to admit. I'm no psychiatrist, but I sensed she was bored. You see, the really fun part of her job was over. (Also, the embarrassing part.) The costumes were finished. All the components of each costume had been made, found, or ordered, and the actors and actresses were wearing them. Mal was no longer needed to scout around for moccasins for an Indian princess, or to fashion a headpiece for a fairy. All she and Savannah had to do now was keep track of the costumes. They made sure they were washed if they got dirty, or repaired if they tore or broke, and that at the end of each rehearsal no part was missing from any costume. Actually, this was a huge and important job. Unfortunately, it was boring, too. And that, as I said, is what I thought was at the root of Mal's problem. But I wasn't sure.

The Monday afternoon rehearsal was especially busy. It was as if *everyone* had suddenly realized we had four days, and only four days, to perfect things. So Claudia was running around touching up her backdrops; the lighting people were going crazy with their fancy equipment; kids who hadn't peeked at a script in weeks were suddenly pouring over them, uncertain about their lines; and Jessi and Ms. Halliday were still rehearsing a couple of the dance routines. All this was going on while Mr. Cheney was directing a rehearsal of the play, from beginning to end.

I was as busy as anyone else. Maybe I didn't have a specific role, but I knew that if I stood back and waited, little jobs (usually little emergencies) would find their way to me.

Sure enough, just after Act I was underway onstage, Carolyn Arnold approached me, her eyes puffy.

"Aren't you supposed to be dancing?" I asked. I glanced at Ms. Halliday, who was putting the rest of the Lost Boys through their paces.

"Yes, but I don't feel good," said Carolyn weakly. I could tell she'd been crying.

I blanched. I hoped she wasn't going to throw up or something.

"What's wrong?"

"My stomach. It hurts."

"What did you eat for lunch?"

"The regular lunch. Then for a snack I had three candy bars."

"Three!" exclaimed Mallory. (I hadn't even seen her approach us.)

"Well, I needed sugar for energy," said Carolyn.

166

"I'll call your mother," offered Mal.

"*I'll* do that," I said.

Carolyn shook her head. "My mother will get mad at me for eating all that junk. Besides, I think I just need to rest. Could I lie down for awhile?"

"Of course," I answered.

"I'll find one of those mats," added Mal.

"Thanks," I replied.

I sat with Carolyn until Mallory dragged a mat and a couple of coats over to us. Carolyn lay down and I covered her with the coats. Then I sat beside her and rubbed her back.

"You stay with Carolyn," Mal whispered to me, "and I'll keep an eye on things. Let me know if you want me to call her mother."

"Okay." I was barely paying attention. Already I had found that from where I was sitting I could tend to Carolyn and keep an eye on the little kids backstage at the same time.

That was probably why, when I caught sight of the triplets having a contest to see who could burp the loudest, I was able to reach them in record time.

"Be right back!" I said to Carolyn as I sprinted across the stage, and I heard her reply, "Okay, thanks. I feel better already."

"Jordan!" I said, speaking as loudly as I could without disturbing the speech Kristy was giving on the other side of the curtain. I was proud of myself for having gotten to the boys so quickly.

But as the word was leaving my lips I heard Mallory exclaim, "Adam!"

Mal and I faced each other. Then Mal turned back to her brothers. "I can't believe you're doing this," she said. "It is so disgusting. Mom won't even let you do it in your own room."

"I learned how to do a juicy burp," spoke up Jordan proudly.

Mal clapped her hand over his mouth. "Don't you dare do one here!"

"Mary Anne?" called Carolyn.

She was sitting up on the mat, and I ran to her. "Do you need to get to the bathroom?" I asked her.

"No. I feel fine. Can I go back to my group now?"

"Are you sure you want to? They're still dancing."

"I can dance. Honest."

"Okay. Go ahead."

I started to return to the triplets, but Mallory was still talking to them, and anyway Act I ended, and Karen marched offstage, looking cross.

"What's the matter?" I asked her.

"Tinker Bell is supposed to tinkle," she replied.

I tried not to smile. "Excuse me?" I said.

"She's supposed to tinkle when she's moving around. Like in the movie. Tinker Bell tells things to Peter Pan, but not in words. When she talks these lights flash and you hear this tinkle, tinkle, tinkle. Why aren't there lights and tinkling for *me*?"

"Because in our play people can *see* you. Remember, you *wanted* to be a real fairy."

"But I still can't talk. I don't have any lines. . . . I WANT — "

"SHH!"

From out of nowhere, Mallory had appeared. I looked around for the triplets. They were no longer burping. They were examining the sprinkler system.

"Shh," hissed Mal again, but more quietly.

"Act Two hasn't even started," said Karen.

"It's going to any minute," replied Mallory.

"Mary Anne, please tell Mr. Cheney I want tinkling when I move around. I want someone behind the curtain to play a triangle," said Karen. "See, I will go leaping across the stage and the people will hear ding, ding, ding! And then maybe the spotlight could blink on and off."

"But, Karen, opening night is — "

"It's four nights away," Mal butted in. "The director can't ask for changes like that now. It's confusing."

"Oh." Karen hung her head.

"But you had a good idea, Karen," I said.

"A great one," added Mal. "Hey, let me show you something. Do you want to look like a true fairy? Then do this."

I started to say, "Mal, I don't think this is the job of the apprentice costume designer," but my attention was drawn to a little scuffle over near the wings. I looked in the direction of the triplets and saw them standing under a shower of water. I raced to them. "What are you doing?" I cried.

"Well . . ." Byron looked more sheepish than either of his brothers. "We made up this raindance, but it didn't look very real, so Adam turned on the sprinklers or something and . . . well . . ." he said again.

Moments later, the water had stopped sprinkling (thanks to Logan) and the rehearsal was continuing, since Mr. Cheney never knew what had happened. Also, Mallory had abandoned Karen and run to the scene of the latest mishap. She stood over her brothers, hands on hips.

"You guys," she said.

"Mal, I think I can handle this," I spoke up.

"But they're my brothers," she replied.

"But you left Karen over there. You just left her."

"You left her, too."

"There wasn't anything for me to do. You keep taking over."

"I what?"

"Every time I turn around, there you are. It's as if you're multiplying, like in *The Sorcerer's Apprentice*."

"I can't help it. I'm a baby-sitter."

"You are the apprentice costume designer. I am the backstage baby-sitter."

"But Mary Anne — "

"Mallory, just let me do my job!" I exploded. Then I handed the triplets a mop, and returned to Karen Brewer.

Mallory

Monday

I don't think I could be in show business as a career. There is just too much pressure. I would be a walking bundle of nerves. Take this play, for example. First, my friends got nervous simply thinking about auditioning. Then they were nervous during the auditions. After the auditions they were nervous waiting to find out whether they had earned the roles they wanted. After the roles were posted, they were nervous about the parts they got. They worried through the rehearsals. And now that opening night is almost here, they're worried about the first performance.

The apprentice costume designer does not escape this worry. I'm just as nervous about opening night as anyone else is. What if the costumes fall apart?

Frankly, I'm not sure why we even bothered to put on a play.

Whoa.

When I reread what I'd written — several days after the *closing* night of *Peter Pan* — I giggled. I must have been in a pretty bad mood when I wrote that. Or else maybe I was just scared. I guess that was it. Mostly, the rehearsals had been fun. They really had been. Sure, we had hit snags, and Cokie had been a prima donna, and Jackie had nearly killed himself trying to fly, but all along we'd been having fun, too. And watching the play come together — watching it grow from a mess of people and scripts and ideas into a fairly smooth performance with costumes and scenery and dancing and singing — was thrilling. It really was.

But by Monday of the week the play would open, everyone certainly was edgy. (And I believe I'm being polite when I use that word.) Mary Anne, for one, was beyond edgy. She went crazy. What did she mean by yelling at me? Well, maybe she didn't exactly yell. Mary Anne rarely does. But when she said, "Just let me do my job!" she was *not* quiet about it. And anyway, she hadn't been doing her job.

Funny. Cokie had accused me of the same thing earlier in the rehearsal. At the time, I didn't know why. Her costume was finished. What was left for me to do? Savannah was helping kids into and out of their costumes.

So I stood around and watched.

For awhile I watched Jessi, which made me sad. She didn't have a lot to do anymore, either. She would run through the dances with the little kids every now and then, but Mr. Cheney and Ms. Halliday were afraid of over-rehearsing them, so Jessi spent a lot of time watching the action onstage from the wings. She didn't smile, just watched.

I wish she had agreed to be a pirate. I know she wanted to be Peter Pan. And she would have done a great job, but Mr. Cheney is right. Jessi is always getting leads in the productions at her ballet school, and not many kids at SMS have ever been in *any* play. Jessi could still have been in *Peter Pan*, though. She would have added to it. More important, she would have had fun. I tried to tell some of this to her, but to be perfectly honest, she has not been easy to talk to lately. Or very pleasant. Maybe later. Maybe I could tell her after the play. I hoped she would cool off by then.

"Hey, Jessi," I said during Act II of the Monday rehearsal.

"Hey," she replied. She was in the wings as usual, positioned so she could see the actors, but not Mr. Cheney. She didn't turn to look at me.

"I think Friday is going to go well, don't you?"

"Yeah, I think so."

"Kristy even knows her lines now," I commented, although Kristy was not speaking at that moment.

"Yup."

"And I think Dawn is going to behave. No more trying to turn the Lost Boys into feminists." I smiled.

"Yeah."

"Do you wish you were in the play now?" I couldn't help asking.

"Why? Do you?"

"Me? No way. I was happy working on the costumes."

Jessi nodded. "They look good, Mal."

"Thanks. . . . Well, do you?"

"Do I what?"

"Never mind." I left Jessi in the wings. Where had my best friend gone? The Jessi who was standing behind me was not the friend I used to know. My old friend would talk to me. When we had problems we discussed them. Together. On the other hand, we had

175

had some fights. But in the end, things always work out. Because we are best friends. Forever friends. Still, I do not like to see my friend hurting.

Mr. Cheney called for a short break and the kids who were onstage ran off. Most of them ran backstage, then headed for the drinking fountains. Cokie ran straight to me.

"Mallory," she exclaimed, looking exasperated, "this costume just is not right. I have decided I hate it."

"What's wrong with it? You loved it before."

"I did not love it. I liked it. But — I don't know — it isn't glamorous."

"Is that all anyone cares about around here?"

Cokie looked taken aback. "What?"

"Nothing. I'm sorry."

"Mallory, it is your job to make me look good."

I glanced around wildly for Savannah or Miss Stanworth, but I couldn't see either one of them. "I've already done my job, Cokie," I said.

Luckily, Mr. Cheney called everyone onstage again. Cokie pouted at me, then left. I heaved a sigh of relief.

There was an awful lot of concern about jobs and whether we were doing them.

176

I sat down on a desk. Where was Ben? Maybe I could talk to him. Ben Hobart is a friend of mine and, yes, he's a boy, but I am not sure he's my boyfriend. We've gone to a few movies and dances, but for heaven's sake, we're eleven years old. I am not ready for commitment. Neither is he. Anyway, Ben was working on the lighting for *Peter Pan*, so he was at every rehearsal, although I didn't see much of him.

Guess what. Maybe Ben and I have ESP or something. Just when I was thinking about him, and wondering where he was, he walked by me.

"Ben!" I called (but not loudly enough for Mr. Cheney to hear).

"Hey, Mal!" he replied. He didn't slow down.

"Ben, can I talk to you?"

"Right now?"

"Well, yeah."

"What's wrong?"

"It's Jessi. She's so sad."

"Let's talk after rehearsal. I'm busy now."

Ben hurried off. Well, *really*.

Act II ended. Act III began. For awhile, I just sat on the desk. I completely ignored everything that was going on around me. I especially ignored Mary Anne, my brothers and sister, and any of the little kids. I had not realized Mary Anne was so touchy about her job, and I was certainly not going to butt in again.

So I sat on the desk and watched David Michael Thomas and Bill Korman tie fourteen pairs of tennis shoes together. When it was time to go home, I'd just let Mary Anne sort out those shoes by herself.

"We could glue them to the floor," I heard Bill say.

"Do you have any glue?" asked David Michael.

"No. I wonder where the art room is in this school."

"It's on the second floor," replied Mary Anne, who I guess had been listening to the conversation, too.

David Michael and Bill craned their necks back and looked up at Mary Anne. "Oops," said Bill.

Mary Anne didn't answer him. She just stood over the boys. And they began to untie the shoes. When the laces were unknotted, she said one word. "Pairs." And the boys paired up the shoes and left them in a neat row.

Mary Anne is not the backstage baby-sitter for nothing.

I continued to sit on the desk. I sat there until Cokie came barrelling off the stage and said, "Mallory Pike, you *aren't* doing your job."

Well, at that moment, I wasn't doing a single thing.

I sighed. "What do you mean?"

"I *knew* my costume looked different. I'm wearing half of Stacey's stuff. Her jewelry. Or something. Plus, I'm missing . . . I don't know . . ."

A horrible, sick feeling washed over me. "Cokie," I said, "stand back for a minute. In the light. Let me look at you."

Cokie did so. "I can't figure out how I put on the wrong things," she said. "You keep all the parts of our costumes together, and this afternoon I put on everything I found."

"Where's Stacey?" I asked.

"Over there." Cokie pointed to Stacey and Sam who were sitting close together (*very* close together) on a pile of tumbling mats.

"Stace?" I called. "Can you come here for a sec, please?"

Well, I don't know how Stacey's costume and Cokie's had gotten mixed up, but somehow they had.

"I *thought* something looked weird," said

Stacey. "But I put on everything in the box marked 'Mrs. Darling.' "

"Maybe you could pay more attention to your job, Mallory," said Cokie, in this voice that crackled with annoyance. "You know, your job is not over. You should help Savannah keep track of the costumes. She can't do it herself. Look. Look over there. What do you see?"

I ignored the fact that Cokie was talking to me the way a teacher might talk to a naughty kindergartner. "I — I see plenty," I replied.

This is what I saw: John's top hat rolling around in a corner. A headdress belonging to one of the Indians lying in a heap near the curtain. Two eyepatches and a plastic sword gathering dust.

Yikes.

I scurried around. In a flash I had gathered up the stray parts to the costumes and put them where they belonged (for instance, on Barry Soeder's head). Then I found Mary Anne.

"I'm really sorry," I told her. "I don't know what got into me. I wasn't doing my job and I wasn't letting you do your job and — and I caused a big mess. You are an excellent backstage baby-sitter."

Then I made Cokie and Stacey stand in front

of me, and I switched things around until they were wearing the proper costumes.

"Now you look glamorous," I told Cokie. "You too, Stacey," I added. (Cokie made a horrible face at Stacey.)

Finally, I found Savannah and apologized to her. My job was not over, after all. On Friday, I would be an important part of our opening night performance.

CHAPTER 19

Jackie

Friday Morning

It is Friday! How did Friday get here so fast? I guess what I am supposed to write about now is Opening Night. That is what tonight is. Only we haven't had opening Night but we have had Dress ~~Rehir Rehair~~ Rehursl. (If you can't spell it out sound it out, but really I think you should use the di~~cshun~~ ~~dik~~ Webster's.)

Oh, Jessi is telling me to write about what happened this morning, so here goes. Our Dress Rehursl.

signed by Jackie Rodowsky

I did not think I would be nervous. I know my lines. I know my dances. I know my songs. I know how to simulate flying. (I still think it is boring, though, and I am now an expert at leaping off of my dresser at home.) But I kept thinking of what could happen tonight. What if I was singing and some spit shot out and everyone saw? What if I opened my mouth to cry, "I'm flying!" and nothing came out, not even any spit?

These things did not happen during our dress rehearsal, but they could have. The dress rehearsal started at eleven o'clock this morning. And of course it took place at SMS because that is where our stage is. *But* eleven o'clock on a Friday morning is during school. (In fact, it is during spelling), so I got to *miss school* to be in the dress rehearsal.

Here is the thing. Everybody at Stoneybrook Elementary missed school during the dress rehearsal. That is because the kids at my school came to watch the dress rehearsal. They were our first audience.

I got to leave school before the rest of my classmates, though. At ten o'clock my teacher said to me, "Jackie, you may get ready to go now."

Then a school bus drove me and my

brother Shea and David Michael Thomas and Nicky Pike and Kerry Bruno and us younger kids over to SMS. We felt very special. As the bus pulled out of the parking lot, one of the Pike triplets (I think it was Adam) shoved his window down and threw his hat out. That was his way of saying, "Yes! Here we go! We are so excited about putting on this play, and now here we are on our way to our first performance in front of a real live audience!"

Unfortunately, the teacher who was riding with us did not know that was what he was doing. She turned around and yelled at Adam. Plus, she made the driver stop the bus so Adam could get off and run back for his hat. When we were on our way again, she made a no talking rule. She should have made a no hat-throwing rule but I guess it was too late for that. We rode the rest of the way to SMS in silence, but we were still excited.

"Now," said the teacher, as the bus stopped at the back door of SMS. (I do not even know that teacher's name. She teaches fifth grade and I am only in second.) "Now please enter the school very, very quietly. Remember that classes are in session. I will lead you to the auditorium."

I felt grown-up walking through the halls of

SMS where the big kids go to school. I tried to make myself look taller.

I felt just a little bit afraid.

But I felt better when we reached the auditorium. There was Mary Anne, my special coach. And there were Kristy and Stacey and Dawn and Jessi and my other friends in the BSC.

"Hi! Hi!" I called. I ran to Mary Anne. I knew we did not have to be so quiet anymore. Luckily, that teacher left. I guess she rode back on the school bus by herself.

"Hi, Jackie," said Mary Anne. "Are you ready for the dress rehearsal?"

I nodded. "Yup."

The reason the kids were going to watch our dress rehearsal is because a dress rehearsal is just about like the real play. We were going to run through it from start to finish without stopping, and we would be in our costumes and makeup and everything. We would have the chance to perform in front of an audience, and the kids wouldn't have to pay to see us.

"Okay, Jackie. I'll help you with your costume now," said Mary Anne.

I took a deep breath.

My costume.

In about half an hour every kid in my whole

school was going to see me onstage in a nightgown.

"Mary Anne? Are you sure I have to wear it?"

Mary Anne looked puzzled. Then she said, "It's a dress rehearsal, Jackie."

"I know. But maybe I could wear a pair of pajamas."

"A pair of pajamas? Your costume is a nightshirt."

"I think it's too big."

"Jackie."

"Okay, okay."

I put on the nightshirt. I wondered how Mary Anne would feel if she had to go on a stage in her underwear. I didn't ask her, though. I could not say "underwear" in front of a girl.

When I was ready I wandered over to the curtain. I stood right behind the crack where it opens. I listened. I could hear voices and footsteps. They were getting louder. I peeked through the opening.

Our audience was arriving.

I was looking at my teacher and the kids in my class and the other teachers and the kindergartners and fifth-graders and all the students in between. And I was wearing a nightgown.

While the other people in the play put on their costumes, I sat under a desk. I would not talk to Mary Anne. But when Mr. Cheney called, "Places, everyone!" I ran to my spot.

Guess what. When I made my entrance on-stage, nobody laughed. Not one person. Maybe because Barry Soeder was wearing his nightshirt, too, and Dawn was wearing her nightgown. I don't know. Or maybe because it was so easy for them to imagine that they were really watching the Darling children in their nursery at nighttime. And they were waiting for Peter Pan to come.

I stopped worrying about my costume. But I didn't stop feeling jittery. I jumped a mile when Kristy appeared in the window. And I jumped another mile when I heard Nana bark. When the curtain closed at the end of Act I, I ran to Mary Anne. I was breathing hard.

"You did great, Jackie!" she cried.

"Thank you. But I'm nervous."

"That's okay. Everyone is."

"I didn't realize what the audience would look like from the stage. All I can see are eyes. Hundreds of them."

"Listen to the applause. You guys are a hit."

"The applause is nice, but my stomach feels funny."

"You have stage fright. That's natural. Okay. Act Two is starting."

I was back onstage before I knew what had happened. I tried not to look at the audience. I tried not to think about the audience. Act II is very complicated, and lots of people are on the stage, or running on and off the stage, so I could not think about anything except my next line or my next step.

Think, think, concentrate, I told myself.

I turned around, ready to —

"Aughhh!" I yelped. (But not very loudly.)

I was facing that crocodile. It was slithering closer to me. I froze. I could not remember what I was supposed to be doing just then. But I did not want that croc anywhere near me.

I stepped toward the croc. I took another step, then another.

I picked up a gray Styrofoam rock (it was part of the scenery) and I bonked the croc over the head with it.

"Hey!" yelled Pete Black. I knew I had not hurt him, but I bet I had surprised him.

For about two seconds no one said anything. I waited for Mr. Cheney to yell at me, but he didn't. This was a true dress rehearsal. We were not going to stop the play for anything. Then the kids in the audience began to laugh.

I had *made* them laugh! It was a nice feeling.

So the next time the crocodile scared me, I threw another fake rock at him. "Cowabunga!" I yelled, and the kids laughed harder. I threw a third rock and yelled "Crocabunga!"

Mr. Cheney was not going to say a word to me.

By the time Act II ended, I had yelled "Crocabunga!" two more times. I really knew how to make that audience laugh.

But when I ran backstage to get ready for Act III, Mr. Cheney was not laughing. Neither was Mary Anne.

"Jackie," said Mr. Cheney, "do you remember the script for *Peter Pan*?"

I frowned. "Yes."

"Does the word 'cowabunga' appear anywhere in it?"

"No. No, sir."

"Does the word 'crocabunga'?"

"No, sir."

"Jackie, if you do anything during Act Three that we have not rehearsed, you may not be in the play tonight. Do you understand?"

"Yes, sir."

"All right. I'll talk to you further at the end of the rehearsal."

"So will I," added Mary Anne.

Bullfrogs. Adults do *not* know how to have fun.

I did not have to be near the crocodile in Act III, so he could not scare me. I think the audience wanted me to say "crocabunga" again. But I did not.

When the play was over, it was time for us to take our bows. Dawn went first, by herself. Then Barry. Then me. (Kristy got to go last, even after the Lost Boys and the pirates and everyone. She is the star.) But when I ran onto the stage, the audience cheered as loudly for me as they did for Kristy later. Some fifth-grade girls even stood up. They gave me a standing ovation! And a bunch of boys yelled, "Crocabunga!"

I grinned until my cheeks hurt.

I was going to be a star myself one day. This was a sign.

So I did not feel too bad when Mr. Cheney snagged me as soon as I ran backstage. "All right, Jackie," he said.

Mr. Cheney gave me a long talk about how we can't play around with the words that Mr. J. M. Barrie wrote. I had heard him say the same thing to Dawn a few weeks earlier. He said "crocabunga" would change the tenor of the play. He said "tenor" so many times I decided I better look it up in Webster's later.

Then Mary Anne talked to me. She did not use big words or tell me about Mr. Barrie. She just said, "Jackie, don't you dare do that tonight. It is not allowed. Absolutely not allowed."

"Okay."

When school was over that day, I ran home.

"How was the play?" Mom asked me.

And I said, "Today was the best day of my entire life."

CHAPTER 20

Claudia

Friday Afternoon

Well, my scenry held up I kept expeting it to fall apart during the dress rehursal this morning. I imaged the back dorps peeling off in strips like wallpaper in a cartoon. Jackie did use one of my foam bolders to wallope Pete Black but that wasnt my fault. I watched some of the play from a seat with the age aibd people, and if I do say so myself the senery looked specticuler. I was still a little nervous about our actual opening night preformance which would start in just a few hours but I was not nerly as nervus as Stacey or dawn or kirsty.

W e did not have a rehearsal on Friday afternoon. Rehearsals were over. (It was hard to believe.) The dress rehearsal had taken place in the morning, our first performance would take place that night, our final performance would take place the next night, and . . . that was it. So much work for two shows. All the tears and sweat and planning and memorizing. The play was almost over and it hadn't even begun.

On Monday, we would start holding our BSC meetings again.

When school ended on Friday, my friends and I walked home together, except for Kristy, who takes the bus. The rest of us stood in the school parking lot and watched her find a seat.

"Get some rest this afternoon!" Stacey called to her through an open window.

"Clear your mind," called Dawn.

"Eat smart," added Mary Anne.

"Yes, Mom," replied Kristy as the bus pulled away from the curb.

"We should take our own advice," I said to Jessi, Mal, Stacey, Dawn, and Mary Anne. "We should spend this afternoon wisely, and use it to get our heads together for tonight." The six of us walked away from school in a pack.

Claudia

"I think we should hang out in your room and pretend this is any ordinary Friday," said Mallory.

"No, we should go to a movie," suggested Stacey.

"I vote for a group nap," said Dawn. "I'm exhausted."

In the end we went off to our separate families, to take individual naps or do whatever would best help each of us relax. Personally, I didn't feel a nap was necessary. I was just going to be in the audience that night, sitting with my parents, my sister, and Russ and Peaches, who are my favorite uncle and aunt.

No one was at home when I let myself into our house. Mom and Dad were at work, and Janine operates on a schedule of her own. She was probably holed up in a library somewhere.

I decided to eat an energy snack, although I wasn't sure why I would need extra energy to sit in an audience all evening. Well, I *was* going to have to arrive at school early to check on the scenery before the show began. I would need energy for that. What gives you energy? I asked myself. Sugar, I replied. And where is the very best place to find sugar? In your bedroom, I said to myself.

I sprinted upstairs and dug an Almond Joy bar from inside my pillowcase. Ahh. Junk food. Dawn was probably at her house biting into a carob bar or something. Carob is just not necessary. If you want to enjoy the flavor of chocolate, then *eat chocolate*. Oh, well. To each his own.

While I ate my candy bar, I talked to Mimi. Mimi was my grandmother. She used to live with us. Mimi and I loved each other so much. She understood me and I understood her. Mimi never yelled. But after she had her stroke, she changed. And awhile later she died. I thought I would never stop feeling sad. Also, I was afraid I would forget what Mimi looked like. So I hung a portrait of her in my room. I had painted the portrait myself. Now I can look at Mimi whenever I want. Sometimes I talk to her.

It is quite helpful.

"Hi, Mimi," I said. "Excuse the candy bar. I'll try not to speak with my mouth full. Well, I guess you know what tonight is. It's here at last. Russ and Peaches are coming. I can't wait to see them. Peaches said she got a perm.

"My friends and I are really nervous about tonight. Especially Kristy, Stacey, and Dawn. They're the ones who have to be *in* the play. Logan, too. Kristy is the most nervous of any of us. She's Peter Pan, the lead. But she'll be fine. So will Stace and Dawn.

"We finished the scenery on Monday. Mr. Cheney liked all my ideas. I was scared about my job at first — being in *charge* of the scenery — but now I'm proud of what I did. I especially like the scenery for the nursery. I'm not sure why. But the Home Underground, where the Lost Boys live in Neverland, is pretty cool, too. I think I will be very sad when they strike the sets, Mimi. You know what that means? It's when they strip the stage after the play is over. I don't know what they're going to do with the sets and scenery. If the Home Underground wasn't so big, I'd bring it here and keep it in my bedroom."

I paused. I wished Mimi could answer me. No matter what anyone says about the value of memories, they do not hold a candle to the real, live person. I'd have given anything for Mimi to be sitting in my room then, so I could have talked to her and not her portrait. But she was gone.

"Well," I said, "wish me luck, Mimi. If you're up there floating around somewhere, peek down at the play tonight and look at the sets. I'll be in the audience, so look down at me, too.

"I love you."

I turned away from the portrait. I never know how to end my talks with Mimi. Over and out? *Hasta la vista?* Have a nice day? So usually I just say, "I love you."

I looked at my watch. Four o'clock. I was supposed to be back at school at six. And I was supposed to relax until then.

"Re*lax*?" I said aloud. "Whose bright idea was that?"

I couldn't relax. For one thing, I'd just eaten a candy bar for energy, and I had energy all right. I was getting jittery.

I was so jittery that when the phone rang, I fell off my bed. As soon as I was back on my feet, I grabbed the receiver. I took a deep breath before saying, "Hello, Baby-sitters Club." (I'd started answering my phone that way when we stopped holding meetings. People were calling for sitters pretty much whenever they felt like it.)

"Hi. It's me."

"Hi, Stace."

"Claud? Are you relaxing?"

"Sort of."

"Are you re*laxed*?"

"Not really."

"Me neither."

"Want to come over?"

"So we can be jumpy together?"

I giggled. "Yeah."

"Okay. Be right over."

Stacey was true to her word. Ten minutes later she was running up the stairs and along the hall to my room.

"I just had this horrible thought," she greeted me.

"How horrible? Do I want to hear it?"

"I guess so. I mean, it's scary, not disgusting. Besides, I'm going to tell you anyway." Stacey straddled my desk chair.

I sighed. "Okay. But remember, this is supposed to be a nice, relaxed, stress-free afternoon. Just keep that in mind."

"What if," began Stacey, "there were a blackout in the middle of the play and the lights went off and there were panic in the auditorium?"

"I have several thoughts about that," I replied. "One, you sound like Mary Anne, the demented version. Two, I think you're worrying about blackouts so you won't worry about your part in the play. And three, the school has an emergency generator."

"Oh."

"Hey, Stace, is your father coming tonight?"

"Yup. All the way from New York. He's going to spend the night in a motel, though. I don't know why he won't stay in our guest bedroom. After all, he and Mom were married to each other for years."

"Parents are weird," I said.

The phone rang again. (This time I did not fall off the bed.) "Hello, Baby-sitters Club," I said. "Hi, Mrs. Newton! . . . Yeah, we'll be holding meetings again starting Monday. . . . Wednesday night? I'll check. I'm not sure who'll be available then, but I'll call you back."

Stacey and I looked through the record book, made a couple of calls, and phoned Mrs. Newton back to tell her who'd be sitting. After that, we decided to bring the portable TV into my bedroom so we could relax in front of it and take calls at the same time.

"What's on?" Stacey asked, flipping the channels.

"I don't know. Slow down. We'll find something."

What we found was an old movie from the 1940s. Guess what it was about. Putting on a Broadway play.

"Cool," said Stace.

We watched the star of the movie as she auditioned for the play, earned the lead, and went through rehearsals. Halfway through the opening night performance — which was a gala affair — a piece of scenery fell over, hit the actress on the head, and knocked her unconscious.

"Oh, my lord!" I cried.

"I bet it was sabotage," said Stacey knowingly.

"I don't care what it was. What if that happens tonight? What if the Home Underground collapses on the Lost Boys? What if the nursery set falls over? I don't want to be responsible for killing Kristy."

"Claudia — "

Ring, ring!

The phone again. I grabbed it up. "Hello?" (I was so unnerved, I forgot to say, "Hello, Baby-sitters Club.")

"Claudia? Is that you?"

"Yeah. Who's this?"

"It's Cokie. Listen, Claudia, I've been thinking. You know the backdrop you made for the 'Ugg-a-Wugg' song?"

"Cokie, it is *not* going to fall down. I promise."

"Excuse me? Claudia, you are so — Hang on a sec. I'm getting another call." Cokie put me on hold while I panicked quietly. Then, "Claudia? I have to go. I'll see you tonight." She hung up without saying good-bye.

"Who was that?" Stacey wanted to know.

"It was Cokie. And she's worried about the scenery. Stace, this is eerie. Here we are worrying about the sets killing someone, and then Cokie calls with a question about the sets. Can you imagine if the backdrop did kill her? Everyone would think I had done it on purpose to get rid of her."

"No one would blame you," Stacey replied, smiling.

But I couldn't smile back. And by the time I arrived at school that evening — at six o'clock on the dot — I was a nervous wreck.

CHAPTER 21

Jessi

Friday evening

It just goes to show. You never know what to expect. Or maybe I should say, the things you least expect sometimes happen. Not often, but sometimes. All I'm going to say right here is that what I least expected was that I would be in the play on opening night. But I was. This is how it happened.

I wasn't even going to *go* to opening night. I know it sounds babyish, but I was still angry and upset and hurt, and I just did not feel like going. The rest of my family was going, but I didn't want to. Not even to see my friends, or to see the kids dance after all the rehearsing we'd done. I'd been to the dress rehearsal. That seemed like enough. But on Friday afternoon Ms. Halliday caught up with me at my locker and asked if I'd come to the auditorium at six to be around in case any of the kids had problems, and also to run the Lost Boys through this one dance that had given them trouble at the dress rehearsal.

I said I'd be there.

I did not say I'd be happy about it.

I arrived at the school in my usual bad mood.

"Hey, Jessi," said Mal tentatively. She'd been awfully quiet around me lately, and I couldn't blame her. I wasn't the pleasantest person.

"Hey," I replied. I tried to dredge up something nice to say. All I could come up with was, "Your hair looks good." (Mal had pulled it back with a pale blue ribbon.)

"Thanks. Um, so does yours."

"Thanks."

Jessi

Sheesh. Mal and I sounded like total strangers. I vowed that the second the closing performance was over I would try to behave like a human being again. I did not want to lose my best friend.

Mal walked off in search of Savannah, and I glanced around. Everyone connected with the play was supposed to arrive between six and six-thirty, and sure enough, backstage was already becoming crowded. Dawn and Mary Anne came in, Dawn looking pale. Stacey and Claudia showed up. (Claudia made a dash for this backdrop she'd made, and began to examine it before she'd even taken off her coat.) And in streamed the little kids — Myriah and Jackie and Karen and Nicky and Margo and the triplets and more.

"Lost Boys over here!" I called. "On the double! Bobby, Shea, Linny, Natalie, Bill and Melody, Carolyn, Nicky, Myriah, and David Michael!"

"In our costumes?" asked Nicky.

"No, you can put them on later."

"What?"

"You can put them on LATER!" I yelled. Backstage was not only crowded, it was noisy.

"Hey, Kristy! Come here!" yelled Barry Soeder.

"Careful! Look out!" said Ben Hobart as he

walked by with a huge piece of equipment.

"Telephone, Mr. Cheney!" called someone.

"Where's Pete?" asked someone else.

I gathered the Lost Boys into an area of the wings that was slightly quieter. At least we weren't tripping over people. "All right, kids. Try to pay attention," I said. "I know it's hard, but concentrate, okay? We're going to begin with — "

"Excuse me, Jessi." Ms. Halliday had joined us. "Sorry to interrupt. Mr. Cheney needs to talk to you. I'll work with the kids."

Mr. Cheney needed to talk to me? Why? A little knot formed in my stomach. "Okay," I said to Ms. Halliday. I walked backstage and practically bumped into Mr. Cheney.

"Oh, Jessi. Good. There you are," he said. "Listen, Pete Black just called. Actually, his mother did. Pete had an accident after school today."

"He did?" I said. (That word "accident" makes my stomach flip-flop.)

"He fell off his bicycle, and he broke his nose."

"Oh, no!"

"He's going to be all right," said Mr. Cheney, "but he won't be able to be in the show tonight. He may not be able to be in it tomorrow night, either. Jessi, could you please play Nana and the crocodile? You know the roles. You've watched Pete dozens of times."

"Me? What about Jason Henderson or one of the other understudies?"

"Jessi, they all have parts in the play. They're pirates, mostly. You know that. And I think they'd like to play those parts. I hadn't counted on needing an understudy for Pete Black. Couldn't you *please* take over for him?"

I didn't know what to say to Mr. Cheney. I certainly couldn't tell him what I was thinking. Because I was thinking, Jessi Ramsey in a non-speaking, nondancing role? After I bragged to the world that I was going to be Peter Pan himself? No, it was just too humiliating.

"Jessi?" said Mr. Cheney.

"Can I think it over?"

Mr. Cheney looked at his watch. "There's only an hour until curtain time, Jessi. How long do you need?"

I sighed. "I guess I don't need any time after all. I'll do it. I'll be Nana and the crocodile."

Mr. Cheney beamed. "Thank you, Jessi. You better go find Savannah and Mallory right away. They'll have to make sure you fit the costumes. And I'll tell the cast about this last-minute change. I'm sorry this won't get into the program."

"That's okay," I said, remembering that I

wasn't listed in the program anyway.

Mr. Cheney left, and I spotted Mallory. "Hey, Mal!" I called. "Mal!" I ran to her. "You won't believe this, but Pete Black broke his nose and he can't be in the play tonight, so I'm going to be Nana and the crocodile."

"You're kidding!"

"Nope. Mr. Cheney told me to try on the costumes."

Mallory looked a whole lot more excited than I felt. "Well, come on!" she cried. "We'll put you in Nana first. Savannah? Savannah?"

Mal and Savannah stuffed me into the dog outfit and then into the croc outfit. Those costumes were *hot* and *heavy*.

"Try slithering," said Mallory when I was in the crocodile costume.

I moved my arms and legs the way I had seen Pete do it.

"Now see how fast you can go."

I skittered along the floor. I was not as fast as Pete, but I guessed I would do. Anyway, I was better than nothing.

"Hey, you have to call your parents!" said Mal. "They ought to know who's going to be inside these costumes tonight."

"Oh, you're right," I replied, struggling out of the croc. I ran for the pay phone, which

was in the hallway near Cokie's star mop closet. By the time I got off the phone, I actually felt a teensy bit excited.

"Jessi!" called Mary Anne, the second I returned backstage. "Come here! I have an idea. Can you put on the crocodile costume again?"

"Now?" I replied. "Why?"

"Just put it on."

Mallory and Savannah stuffed me back into the costume. "Now what?" I asked.

I heard Mary Anne say, "Okay, Jackie. Turn around," and I peered out through the croc's slitted mouth in time to see Jackie Rodowsky catch sight of me and let out a yelp.

"That was mean, Mary Anne!" he exclaimed.

"Calm down," said Mary Anne evenly. Then she leaned over and rapped on the crocodile's snout. "Open up!" she commanded.

I opened the jaws of the costume. "Hi, Jackie," I said.

"Jessi!" he cried.

"Pete Black isn't feeling well," Mary Anne explained to Jackie, "so he won't be here tonight. Jessi's taking his place. She'll be inside the crocodile costume tonight."

"Jessi will?" repeated Jackie. "Oh, I feel so much better!"

Kristy

Friday Night

I don't know when I have felt so nervous. Maybe not ever before in my life. Because I have never had to stand on a stage in front of a large crowd of people and sing. Well, actually, I did do that just this morning, but this morning wasn't so bad because the audience was a bunch of kids. And some teachers, of course. But just knowing we were performing in a dress rehearsal and not on opening night made a big difference. That and the fact that people hadn't paid to see us. Tonight the audience would pay good money to come to our performance. What if they weren't satisfied? What if I forgot all my lines and my voice cracked while I was singing and the audience demanded a refund and we didn't even get to have a closing night performance because opening night was a flop?

Those were the healthy thoughts running through my mind when I arrived at SMS on Friday evening for the opening night performance of *Peter Pan*. Charlie drove Sam, David Michael, Karen, and me to school at six o'clock.

"I'll be back later with the rest of the family," he said as he dropped us off at the main entrance. "Break a leg!"

"Break a *leg*?" repeated David Michael. He looked insulted.

"It means good luck," Karen told him. "Everyone knows that."

"Well, *I* didn't — "

"You guys, *please*," I said, as I watched the taillights of Charlie's car disappear around a curve. "Give me some peace." I paused. "Hey, Sam," I continued, "take Karen and David Michael backstage, all right? I'll be there in a few minutes."

Sam shrugged his shoulders. "Okay."

I waited until Sam led them off. Then I tip-
toed to the foyer at the entrance to the auditorium. The foyer was empty of people. Two
desks had been set up and on each one sat a
stack of programs for *Peter Pan*. I picked one
up and glanced through it. It looked professional. Almost like a *Playbill* for a Broadway
show in New York City. I set it back on the
stack. Then I looked at the posters advertising
the play. I looked at the sign over the spot
where the ticket-seller would be sitting. I
groaned. We should have put on a free play.
That would have taken off some of the
pressure.

After a moment I stepped into the auditorium itself. From behind the curtain I could
hear mumblings and scufflings. I could see the
shadows of feet as people hurried back and
forth. But the auditorium was still and de-
serted. I squinted my eyes and pictured the
way it would look in just an hour and a half.
It would be brimming over with people waiting for the lights to dim, expectant, and maybe
a little nervous because their sons or daughters
or brothers or sisters or friends would soon
be on the stage. My family would occupy
about half a row: Mom, Nannie, Watson,
Charlie, Andrew, and Emily Michelle. Also
Bart Taylor. He was coming to the play with

my family. (He doesn't go to SMS.) In other rows in other parts of the auditorium would be Claudia and her sister and parents, Mary Anne and her dad and Dawn's mom, Mallory and her clan, and basically most of Stoneybrook.

"If I make a mistake tonight," I muttered, "half the town will witness it."

I left the auditorium quickly. I ran back outside, gulped in some fresh cold air, then returned to the school. I took the long way to the backstage entrance. I passed Cokie's dressing room.

As I did, the door opened, causing the yellow star to flop back and forth.

"Hi, Kristy," said Cokie.

"Hi."

Cokie was dressed and in full makeup. She was ready for the play. "How do I look?" she asked, twirling around.

"Fine."

"And it's all due to me, her personal makeup artist," said someone from inside the closet. The voice was unpleasantly familiar.

I peeked into the closet. There was Grace Blume. "You're Cokie's makeup artist?" I repeated. Unbelievable.

"It's the only way to go," said Cokie. "When I'm onstage tonight, I won't have to worry about how I look. I can concentrate solely on my lines. I guess you'll have to concentrate pretty hard on your lines, too, won't you, Kristy?''

"What do you mean?''

"Just that it took you so long to memorize them in the first place. And most people suffer from stage fright, especially on opening night. So between that and your fuzzy grasp of your material, well . . .''

"Well, break a leg, Kristy,'' said Grace from the closet. Then she snorted.

I tried to think of a snappy comeback, but I couldn't. So I just walked away. However, when I ran into Dawn backstage, I exploded.

"Cokie and Grace are jerks, total jerks!'' I cried.

"So what else is new?''

"They're trying to psych me out so I'll mess up. Dawn, you don't think I'm going to forget all my lines tonight, do you?''

"All of them?'' said Dawn. "No.''

"Dawn!''

"I'm teasing. Lighten up. What did Cokie and Grace do?''

I told her, then said, "Isn't that a psych-out? Isn't it?''

Dawn sighed. "I guess. Listen, I'm nervous

tonight, too. In fact . . . in fact, my stomach doesn't feel so good."

"Uh-oh. Did you eat something unusually weird for dinner?" I asked.

"Eat? I couldn't eat. I haven't eaten all day."

"Oh, great. Dawn, that's why you don't feel well. You have to eat something. If you don't, you're going to faint. Tonight. Onstage."

Dawn moaned. "I *can't* eat."

"Mary Anne!" I called. "Mary Anne, come here!"

Mary Anne approached us, followed by the crocodile.

"Pete, go away," I said crossly. "This is girl talk."

Mary Anne giggled.

So did the crocodile. Then he opened his great green jaws. "Hi, you guys!"

"Jessi! What are you doing in there?" exclaimed Dawn, peering into the costume. "You better get out. Pete'll kill you."

"No, he won't," replied Jessi. "I'm Pete tonight. I mean, I'm Nana and the crocodile. Pete broke his nose this afternoon."

"You're kidding!" I cried. "*You're* going to be inside those costumes, Jessi?"

"Yes," answered her muffled voice.

"Kristy?" said Mary Anne. "You called me?"

"Oh, yeah. Would you please do something about your sister? She just told me she hasn't eaten all day and now she doesn't feel well. If she faints while we're onstage together tonight, I'll — I'll — Well, she can't do that to me. I have enough to worry about."

"Do that to *you*?" cried Dawn. "*I'm* the one who's going to be fainting onstage."

"Oh, cut it out, you guys," said Jessi. "You're just nervous. Everyone stop talking and take three slow, deep breaths. You, too, Mary Anne. We all need to relax." We breathed. "Good," said Jessi. "Now go on about your business." She snapped her jaws shut and slithered off to find Mallory and Savannah so she could change into the Nana costume for Act I.

The time passed more quickly than I had thought it would. I put on my costume. I put on my makeup. Mary Anne made Dawn eat a package of crackers from the snack machine outside the cafeteria. On one side of the heavy red curtains across the stage, the cast and crew readied themselves for the moment when that curtain would open. On the other side, the audience gathered.

Once, I stepped up to the curtain to peek through the slit.

"Don't," whispered Jessi. "That makes it worse."

"I want to know what I'm in for," I said.

"It's better not to know. When you go on-stage, pretend you have no audience at all. Pretend the auditorium is empty."

"Okay."

Before I knew it, Mr. Cheney was standing on the stage, welcoming the audience to the opening night performance of *Peter Pan*. When he finished, the curtain parted. The audience clapped loudly.

And the show began.

Dawn and I stood in the wings for a few moments, holding hands until she made her entrance. Then Karen and I stood together waiting to make *our* entrance. I was glad I didn't have to appear on that windowsill all by myself. Karen, in her Tinker Bell costume, would be a great comfort.

"Ready?" I whispered as we listened for our cue.

"Ready."

We leaped onto the sill. The audience was hushed. There were Dawn and Jackie and Barry, pretending to be asleep in their beds.

And there, dead ahead, was the entire audience. How could I pretend it wasn't there when it spread away from me, row after row after row?

I forgot my first line. What was I supposed to say? I couldn't think of a single thing. Karen glanced up at me, but she didn't speak, I guess remembering what had happened the last time she tried to help me. My eyes met with Dawn's. She didn't speak, either. Everyone would have noticed.

I nearly burst into tears. Then I caught sight of a movement out in the wings. Jessi was there in the Nana costume. She opened the dog's mouth and she whispered my line loudly.

I repeated it.

I didn't forget a single thing after that. Not one word. Not from then until we were taking our curtain call. In fact, during the "Ugg-a-Wugg" song, I felt confident enough to smile charmingly at Cokie. We were onstage with Dawn and all the little kids — the Lost Boys and Indians. As the song began, I grinned at her. It was my way of saying, "You couldn't psych me out, Cokie. You couldn't do it. When will you learn?"

Then, as we approached Cokie's first solo line in the song, a wonderful, hideous idea came to me. I sang along with Cokie, right through her line. And through every other line Cokie was supposed to sing alone. I did a wonderful job. I knew Cokie's part as well as my own.

"What are you doing?" she hissed at one point during the song.

"I'm sorry," I hissed back. "I'm just all confused. You know, a little fuzzy about my material."

Cokie tossed her head and continued the song. So did I. Her parts and my parts. At the end of Act II, Mr. Cheney pulled me aside backstage. "You're doing splendidly, Kristy, splendidly. I'm very proud of you. But you fell down a little during 'Ugg-a-Wugg.' You'll have to work on that tomorrow."

"Yes, sir. Sorry," I said.

When the curtain parted and the final act began, I barely felt nervous. Just exhilarated. I was having a great time. The time of my life.

CHAPTER 23

Dawn

Friday Night

I guess not eating all day Friday wasn't the brightest thing I could have done. But I had this fear - and I don't know where it came from - that when I got on the stage in front of the audience I would be so nervous I would barf. And not only would everyone see me barf, but then the performance would have to be stopped while Mr. Halprin mopped up the stage, and Mr. Cheney sprayed around disinfectant and air freshener. (The good part about this scenario was that Cokie probably wouldn't want to use her dressing room after Mr. Halprin finished cleaning up.)

Anyway, I decided that the best way not to barf on the stage would be to perform on an empty stomach. That way, there wouldn't be anything to barf up, which is why I didn't eat all day....

I don't know if I've ever told this to anyone before, but I don't like to be the center of attention. At least I don't think I do. I'm not shy; not like Mary Anne. It's just that people so often seem to *need* me. I'm better at being a helper and quietly following along with things than I am at standing out and saying, "I'm here! Pay attention to me!" Not that I follow the crowd, either. I do things my own way, but I usually do them quietly. And when my parents (I mean my mom and my dad, not my mom and my stepfather) are having problems I'm there for them to lean on. When my brother is upset about the divorce I'm there for *him* to lean on. When Mary Anne is having trouble with Logan I'm there for *her* to lean on. See? I'm not a follower, but I'm in the background a lot of the time. And I like it that way. Or I thought I liked it that way.

Which was one reason I began to feel nervous about the opening night performance. Who am I to want to shine? I asked myself. Why did I set myself up to be the center of attention? (Okay, Kristy was the *real* center of attention, but I did have a leading part in the play.) Why had I done this to myself? I should have stayed in the background. I'm usually needed in the background. I'm good at being there.

Basically, I talked myself into being extra nervous for opening night. Even though the dress rehearsal went fine, I decided that maybe I should skip lunch that day. Then in the afternoon I realized I was a teeny bit queasy. So I didn't eat a snack when I came home from school. And the queasiness did not go away. I worried more and more about puking onstage, so of course I didn't eat supper, either.

By the time Mary Anne and I had returned to SMS to get ready for the performance, I felt as if I were going to faint. I hadn't intended to tell that to anyone, but when I was talking to Kristy, it slipped out. And Kristy had a fit. She told Mary Anne to do something about me.

"Did you even eat breakfast this morning?" asked Mary Anne as she marched me off to the vending machine. "You didn't, did you?

I don't remember seeing you eat anything."

"I had a rice cake," I said truthfully. "You were in the bathroom then."

Mary Anne grunted.

We stopped in front of the machine and looked over the possibilities.

"You should eat something with sugar in it," said Mary Anne.

"No way. I'm not that desperate."

"All right. Then how about peanut butter crackers? They'll fill you up and they're full of protein."

"Probably chemicals and additives, too."

"One package isn't going to kill you. Besides, do you want to faint tonight?"

"No. I want to be a star."

"You will be, you know," said Mary Anne. "You keep joking about that, but Mr. Cheney cast you as Wendy for a reason. And you're doing a great job. You haven't even rewritten J. M. Barrie's lines lately."

"And when I did," I replied, watching the package drop into the bin, "I never said anything as wild as crocabunga."

Mary Anne laughed. "Now eat your crackers, calm down, and we'll go back to the stage. I'll help you with your makeup."

The crackers tasted chemically and felt gritty, but I ate all of them, and had to admit when I finished, that I felt better. I put on my costume and Mallory checked me over. Then I put on my makeup. I was standing in front of a mirror between Kristy and Stacey. Mary Anne was behind us.

"Feel better?" Kristy asked me.

"What's wrong?" Stacey wanted to know.

"My stomach. I didn't eat all day." I watched Stacey's eyes grow wide, and knew what she was thinking. "My stomach is fine *now*. I needed to eat. I am *not* going to barf, Stace." Stacey cannot stand barfing or anything remotely connected to it. "I was nervous, that's all."

"You know what?" said Kristy a moment later. "This is so silly, but I wish my father were here tonight. I wish he could see me."

"That's not silly," said Stacey.

"I mean, I haven't seen him in years. Why should tonight suddenly be so important? My mom's here."

"I wish my dad were here, too," I said. "He'd never have believed it. *Me*, onstage. I didn't even tell him about the play, though. He'd feel bad he was missing it. I'll send him the program, maybe."

"Boy. Now I feel lucky," said Stacey. "I was complaining because my dad's going to be here tonight, but he won't stay with us. He's staying in a motel. I guess I should be glad he's here at all."

The three of us looked at each other in the mirror. I felt a sob rise into my throat. *"Don't cry, you guys. We cannot cry. Not now. Our makeup will run and we'll have to start over."*

So we hugged each other instead.

The hug fortified me. (It was much better than crackers.) When Mr. Cheney gathered Jackie and Barry and me so we could wait to make our entrance, I didn't have a heart attack or faint or barf or anything. I walked onto the stage and was instantly transported into the story of *Peter Pan*. The audience was already transported. They had found themselves looking at Claud's set when the curtains parted, and now the three Darling children were before them. The audience was in an English nursery decades ago. So was I. All thoughts of suggesting that Peter learn to sew or that the Lost Boys learn to cook left my mind. I wasn't there to teach the audience a lesson. I was there to present to them a fairy tale with which they were already familiar and which was comforting because it was familiar. And for those children watching it for the first time, well, I had to hope they would enjoy the magic and drama and energy, and learn from some other story that boys can cook and sew as well as girls, and girls can have adventures as exciting as boys'.

Those thoughts swarmed through my head in, like, a tenth of a second. Trust me, I could not think about much of anything aside from the play. I concentrated so hard, people could probably *see* me concentrating. At first. But by the time we had finished singing "Tender Shepherd" I was caught up in the story and I just floated through it. I *was* the story.

I was Wendy.

And guess what. I liked being the center of attention. I liked making the audience happy. I liked making the children laugh.

When the curtains closed at the end of the last act, I burst into tears. I was happy and sad and relieved and confused.

"Prepare for curtain calls!" said Mr. Cheney, harried as usual. "You were splendid tonight, kids. Every single one of you."

Through my tears I glimpsed the curtain parting again. "Go on, Dawn," said Stacey. "You're first."

I returned to the stage, alone this time. The audience was clapping so loudly that the sound echoed off the walls. Somehow I caught sight of Mary Anne in that huge crowd, and she waved to me. Then I moved to one end of the stage while the rest of the cast took their bows. When we were assembled in one large group, Mr. Cheney took a bow.

I was about to turn and lead everyone off into the wings when I saw someone from the audience make his way up the steps to the stage, and then over to Kristy.

It was Bart. He handed her flowers and she burst into tears.

Charlie Thomas followed Bart with more flowers for Kristy and a small bouquet for Karen, too.

Once again I almost left the stage, but Barry Soeder grabbed my hand and pulled me back. Mary Anne's father, my stepfather, was approaching. He handed me a dozen roses.

"Congratulations, Dawn," he said. "I'm so proud of you." Then he slipped something else into my hand. I looked down. It was a videocassette. "I taped the play, the entire play," Richard told me. "You can send this to your dad. Then he won't miss your performance after all."

When the curtain closed for the last time, backstage became a sea of crying, hugging, laughing cast members who were soon joined by their crying, hugging, laughing families and the crying, hugging, laughing crew. Sam kissed Stacey in front of everyone. Bart kissed

Kristy. Jackie shouted, "Crocabunga!" (which he had *not* done during the play). And Jessi let her little sister try on the crocodile costume.

When I went to bed that night, I dreamed of roses and clapping hands.

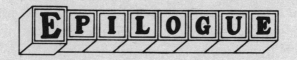

EPILOGUE

The S M S Express

February issue
Peter Pan was
a labor of love.
That is what
this reporter learned
when on assignment
for the S M S
Express. Putting
on the play
meant hard work
and a few tears
and long hours —
because everyone
wanted the show
to be a success.
Peter Pan, which
was performed

on the nights of January 24th and 25th, took in almost $1,000. That was enough to cover the cost of putting on the play — with some left over. The profits were donated to three nearby soup kitchens to help feed hungry people in our area.

For this reporter, the official beginning of the production was the day the posters appeared in school, announcing the upcoming tryouts for the play...

Well, it's over. And I mean, really over. *Peter Pan* has opened and closed. The scenery has been taken down and put away. So have the costumes, except for the special ones like Nana and the crocodile which were rented from someplace in Stamford. They were returned the Monday after closing night. I wish they were a little closer at hand. I got sort of attached to them in the two nights I wore them. After all my griping, after my temper tantrums and bad moods, you know what I discovered? That I really did want to be in the play. I should have taken up Mr. Cheney's offer to be a pirate from the start. Plus, I guess it's true. I am a great dancer, but maybe I am not such a hot singer or actress. Yet. Oh, well. Live and learn. In the end, I made up with all my friends, *and* had a terrific time playing Nana and the croc. I'm only sorry Pete Black had to break his nose in order for me to learn these lessons. But he says there will be other plays.

Pete has his head screwed on straight, no matter what Kristy's opinion of him might be.

Anyway, as you can see, I finished the article. I handed it in to Emily Bernstein, and a couple of weeks later it was printed in our school paper. When I first sat down to write the rough draft, my friends gave me a hand once again. I asked them for their final thoughts and observations. This is what they wrote:

I am so proud of all you guys! The play was wonderful. I'm glad I was able to have a small part in it.
— Mary Anne

I MAY NEVER BE A PROFESSIONAL ACTOR, BUT I SURE HAD FUN PLAYING NOODLER. (HARDLY ANYONE EVEN REALIZED THAT WAS MY NAME, UNLESS THEY COMBED THE PROGRAM.)
—LOGAN

Hey, Stace, you want to go out Friday night? Oh, sorry, Jessi.... And so Mr. and Mrs. Darling waltzed into the future and lived happily ever after.
—Sam

What can I say. My scenery didn't kill anyone.
— Claudia

Jessi

I said all my lines like I was
supost to and I'm very glad Jessi
was the crocodile.
           — signed by Jackie Rodowsky

KRISTY, I'M GOING TO GET YOU. BEWARE.
REVENGE IS SWEET.
               —COKIE

Ha. You don't frighten me. Now on
to important things. I decided I
wanted my father to know about the
play, so I asked Mom to send him a
program. Mom's trying to find out
where he is, exactly. I'm not getting
my hopes up. Anyway, I'm just happy
to have been in the play.
              —Kristy

My dad received the videotape.
He said he cried when he
watched the play. He said he
hoped we'll never have to have
secrets from each other. —Dawn

I feel spoiled. My dad got to see the play for himself. He still stayed in the motel, but that's okay. He and Mom sat together in the audience and no blood was shed.

Yes, Sam, of course I want to go out Friday night!
—Mrs. Darling

Oh, my lord! Where's my measuring tape? Please, oh, please tell me I didn't leave it hanging around Captain Hook's waist. —Mal

About the Author

ANN M. MARTIN did *a lot* of baby-sitting when she was growing up in Princeton, New Jersey. She is a former editor of books for children, and was graduated from Smith College.

Ms. Martin lives in New York City with her cats, Mouse and Rosie. She likes ice cream and *I Love Lucy*; and she hates to cook.

Ann Martin's Apple Paperbacks include *Yours Turly, Shirley; Ten Kids, No Pets; With You and Without You; Bummer Summer;* and all the other books in the Baby-sitters Club series.

THE BABY-SITTERS CLUB®

by Ann M. Martin

More titles... ▶

The Baby-sitters Club titles continued...

Available wherever you buy books...or use this order form.

Scholastic Inc., P.O. Box 7502, 2931 E. McCarty Street, Jefferson City, MO 65102

Please send me the books I have checked above. I am enclosing $_____
(please add $2.00 to cover shipping and handling). Send check or money order - no
cash or C.O.D.s please.

Name _____

Address _____

City_____ State/Zip _____
Please allow four to six weeks for delivery. Offer good in the U.S. only. Sorry, mail orders are not
available to residents of Canada. Prices subject to change.

It's a Super Special Month!

YOU CAN WIN A TRIP TO WALT DISNEY WORLD RESORT®!

© 1992 Walt Disney Company.

Enter The Winter Super Special Giveaway for The Baby-sitters Club® and Baby-sitters Little Sister® fans!

Visit Walt Disney World Resort...and experience all the excitement of Peter Pan, Tinkerbell, and a whole cast of characters! We'll send the **Grand Prize Winner** of this Giveaway and his/her parent or guardian (age 21 or older) on an all-expense paid trip, for 5 days and 4 nights, to Walt Disney World Resort in Florida!

10 Second Prize Winners get a Baby-sitters Club Record Album!
25 Third Prize Winners get a Baby-sitters Club T-shirt!

Early Bird Bonus!
100 early entries will receive a Baby-sitters Club calendar! But hurry!
To qualify, your entry must be postmarked by December 1, 1992.

Just fill in the coupon below or write the information on a 3" x 5" piece of paper and mail to:
THE WINTER SUPER SPECIAL GIVEAWAY, P.O. Box 7500, Jefferson City, MO 65102.
Return by March 31, 1993.

Rules: Entries must be postmarked by March 31, 1993. Winners will be picked at random and notified by mail. No purchase necessary. Valid only in the U.S. Void where prohibited. Taxes on prizes are the responsibility of the winners and their immediate families. Employees of Scholastic Inc.; its agencies, affiliates, subsidiaries; and their immediate families are not eligible. For a complete list of winners, send a self-addressed stamped envelope after March 31, 1993 to: The Winter Super Special Giveaway Winners List, at the address provided above.

The Winter Super Special Giveaway

Name _____ Age _____

Street _____

City _____ State/Zip _____

Where did you buy this book?

☐ Bookstore   ☐ Drugstore   ☐ Supermarket   ☐ Library
☐ Book Club   ☐ Book Fair   ☐ Other_____(specify)   BSC692